Other People's Showers

Other People's Showers

MARK PATERSON

TORONTO

Exile Editions

2003

This edition is published by Exile Editions Limited,
20 Dale Avenue, Toronto, Ontario, Canada M4W 1K4

Sales Distribution:
McArthur & Company
c/o Harper Collins
1995 Markham Road
Toronto, ON
M1B 5M8
toll free:
1 800 387 0117
(fax) 1 800 668 5788

Composition & Design by *Michael P. Callaghan*
Typeset at *Moons of Jupiter, Toronto ON*
Printed and Bound at *Gauvin Imprimerie, Hull QC*

The publisher wishes to acknowledge
the assistance toward publication of
the Canada Council and the Ontario Arts Council.

ISBN 1-55096-567-0

For Lynn, Cate, and Anika

CONTENTS

SATURDAY NIGHT

Dimitri was hiding behind the washing machine again.

Beth-Ann slipped her quarters into the slots and pushed them in. As the water filled, she dropped her clothes into the washer. She scooped detergent into her plastic measuring cup. And she ignored Dimitri. Pretended she didn't know he was there; pretended she couldn't hear him breathing behind the washing machine.

Beth-Ann sprinkled the detergent on her clothes and closed the lid. She counted her change for the dryer, for later. She told herself to stop stalling, that she could count her change upstairs, in her apartment. She told herself to hurry; she had timed her wash to start at the beginning of the nine-thirty television shows and was going to miss all of the opening sequences if she didn't hustle.

She bit the edge of her thumbnail. She reached back into the box of detergent and grabbed a little cluster of soap crystals with the tips of her fingers. She flung them casually behind the washer and walked quickly to the elevator.

There wasn't much room behind the washing machine. Dimitri's back pressed hard against the wall, and his drawn up thighs pressed hard against his stomach and chest. His arms were wrapped around his bent knees, hands clasped together. The toes of his running shoes bent backwards against the machine's back panel. His neck curled forward, keeping his head from touching the black rubber water hoses. Remaining in this position for long periods of time caused Dimitri to breathe loudly.

It was dirty behind the washing machine. And dusty. Balls of lint — grey ones, yellow ones, baby blue ones — lay on the concrete floor in the small space between the machine and the wall. White paint chips were scattered like confetti. One lonely black sock, riddled with dust and lint, rested on the ground. An abandoned-looking cobweb was spun between the washer and dryer, down near the floor, only a few detergent crystals snared. Behind the washing machine, Dimitri inhaled dust, and it made him wheeze quietly.

He pushed himself up, feeling the cracks in the wall pass against his back, until he was standing. He stretched his arms and neck. He twiddled his toes inside his shoes. He brushed the front of his shirt off, creating a small cloud of dust and lint and paint chips. He sidestepped to the right, and came out from behind the washing machine. He crawled into the dryer and waited.

Beth-Ann returned to the basement during the commercial break between the end of the nine-thirty shows and the beginning of the ten o'clock shows. Half-hour programs were for washing, hour-long programs were for drying — the timing was impeccable. Beth-Ann had exactly three minutes and thirty seconds to go downstairs, stuff her wet clothes in the dryer, place the coins, start the machine, and dash back upstairs again. After that, she would have an hour to stretch out on the couch with a bag of vinegar chips and a bottle of Pepsi, free to flip back and forth between the worlds of warriors, barbarians, and Texas rangers. So intent on making it back on time, she nearly forgot about Dimitri.

But as soon as she saw the washing machine, white and dormant and waiting to be emptied, Beth-Ann remembered.

She felt suddenly conspicuous, as if it was she who was hiding and not Dimitri; as if behind the washing machine was a normal place to dwell and she was strange for walking around in large and open spaces. She listened intently. No breathing.

Beth-Ann placed her hands firmly on top of the washing machine. She pressed her toes against the floor. As her body rose, so did her heart rate; she was prepared to be startled but still felt scared. She wondered if it was better to know, or better to be snuck up on. She felt a wave of pleasant sickness crawl across her abdomen as she strained to look over the dial panel of the machine.

But there was nothing behind it. No blue Dimitri eyes, bright like a Husky's; no dark and straight-combed Dimitri hair, black like a crow's feathers. Only dust and lint and hoses and one black sock. Beth-Ann couldn't help but feel disappointed.

After deciding the sock was definitely not hers, she began to hurry. She opened the washer and grabbed a large clump of cold, wet clothes. Holding them against her chest with one hand, she bent and opened the dryer door with the other.

"OOGAH-OOGAH-OOGAH!"

Beth-Ann screamed, a short, high-pitched yelp. She dropped her clean clothes on the floor. Her heart beat in her throat, and she could feel the pulse in her temples without touching them. Maybe getting snuck up on *was* better.

Dimitri was curled up inside the dryer like a folded sock, lying in a ball with his arms wrapped around his bent knees. His body filled the entire drum. He turned his head a little to the side, and through the mixed-up mess of arms and legs and hands and feet, his eyes met Beth-Ann's. "Oogah?" he said quietly, sweetly, as if asking if she was okay.

"That wasn't nice," Beth-Ann scolded, making the best angry face she could.

"Sorry."

"Come on. Get out of there. I want to do my drying."

Dimitri shifted his body around in the dryer. His head popped out of the opening and he pushed the rest of himself out, falling gently to the floor on his back. He blinked in the light.

Beth-Ann immediately began throwing her wet clothes into the dryer. Damp shirts and soggy pants whipped by Dimitri's nose and chin. He kept an eye open for bras and underwear.

"You're in my way. Move it!"

Dimitri stood up and stretched his limbs. He said, "Here, let me help you."

Beth-Ann stared at him angrily, her brown eyes piercing him. She ran her fingers violently through her long brown hair and held a tuft of bangs aloft. Her furrowed brow obscured the freckles on her forehead. Her frowning lips looked dry. "Just get out of here," she spat. "Get away from me. Asshole."

Dimitri shrugged his shoulders. "Sorry." He turned and drifted off.

Beth-Ann pretended not to watch him traipsing toward the parking garage.

Beth-Ann lay on her back on the couch, her head propped up against two cushions. She couldn't concentrate on her remote. She stuffed her mouth with vinegar chips, a slow but constant procession, and allowed the commercials and boring parts of the television programs to play out on her screen. She wondered if she and Dimitri were the only tenants in their building home tonight; home instead of out at a club or a movie, like normal people on Saturday nights. She told herself it was still early, that she didn't have to stay in all night. She remembered telling herself the same thing the weekend before.

She pictured Dimitri in the dryer, and tried to recreate the split-second of terror she'd felt in the laundry room. It wasn't the same as the real thing.

Her chip bag was empty. She took a big sip of Pepsi. She brushed the chip crumbs off the front of her shirt with the tips of her fingers. She continued brushing her chest even after all the crumbs were gone.

Beth-Ann left the couch after staring at the news for ten inattentive minutes. She stepped quietly out of the elevator into the basement and saw her laundry basket filled with clothes, dry and folded. Her throat felt parched.

She reached into the basket and took one of her T-shirts from the top of the pile. It wasn't folded exactly the way she liked. "But not a bad job for a guy," she thought. She pictured Dimitri folding her clothes, putting his hands all over them. A chill crawled down the back of her neck and spread to her shoulders. She shuddered and her teeth chattered for a second.

Beth-Ann reached slowly for the dryer door, yanked it open. Empty. Of course, she thought, it was still way too hot to go inside. "Hello?" she sang. "Where are you?" Beth-Ann crept past the washing machine and tip-toed around the side. Steadying herself for a fright, she peeked behind it, but saw nothing. Just dust and lint and the one lone sock like before. "Dimitri?" she called. The laundry room was appallingly still, hideously quiet.

Beth-Ann placed her left foot between the back of the washing machine and the wall. She wedged her left hip into the space. The rest of her body followed. She had to duck under the hoses, and allowed her back to slide down against the wall until she was crouching. Her drawn up thighs pushed hard against her stomach and chest. She wrapped her arms around her bent knees and clasped her hands together. She began to breathe loudly. She felt dust in the back of her throat. And she waited.

OTHER PEOPLE'S FUNERALS

We had been going to funerals of strangers for about a year when Kyle Mather's tragic story hit the newspapers. The timing couldn't have been better.

Kyle was to be our first semi-celebrity. While I cooked breakfast, a fat feta cheese and spinach omelet with fried potatoes and onions on the side, Sylvia sat at the kitchen table and read me the highlights from the newspaper. "It says he mistook the washer fluid for leftover booze from a camping trip."

I had my head in the fridge, the sour cream eluding me. "I don't get it."

"It says they went camping in Vermont a week before the dance, during spring break. They bought liquor over there and poured it into empty wiper fluid bottles to sneak back across the border."

"Kids," I said with the sour cream container under my arm, and closed the refrigerator door. I gently flipped the omelet, using two spatulas to make sure it didn't break apart. A little bit off half-raw egg splashed on the front of my robe. I wiped it with a paper towel. "But why did he drink the wiper fluid? I mean, it's blue."

"It says he was already so drunk by the time he got to the dance that he probably didn't notice, or didn't bother to check."

"When's the funeral?"

"Saturday."

I turned off the heat beneath the potatoes and onions and tipped them from the pan into a large shallow bowl, decorated with drawings of various herbs. A wedding gift from Sylvia's Aunt Phoebe (may she rest in peace). "Is there a viewing?" I asked, licking a finger.

"I certainly hope so," Sylvia said. "Let me check."

I felt for the lid of the sour cream with my fingers, my eyes on Sylvia. She was bent over the table, flipping quickly through another section of the paper, looking for the obits. "It might not be in there yet," I offered. She didn't look up. She ran one finger down the open page, her eyes squinted in concentration. Her white robe was open in front, probably a bit more than she thought it was. I could see a good portion of the curve of her right breast. The robe cut diagonally across the light pink outer halo of her nipple. I felt a warm pang inside my own robe. I put the sour cream down on the counter, turned the other stove burner off, and walked toward her.

Before Sylvia could look up, I reached beneath her robe and quietly wrapped my hand around the soft arc of her breast. I squeezed gently. "Thursday and Friday night," she whispered in exhale. I shifted my fingers and her nipple became erect between two of them. "He's exposed Thursday and Friday night," she breathed into my ear, her lips gently biting my lobe with each syllable. I turned her chair around to face me and lifted her from it. She wrapped her legs tightly around my waist, her arms around my neck. "The eggs," she panted, her lips covering mine. Her morning breath was strong; fragrant in some ways and rank in others, with just a slight suggestion of decay. It drove me crazy.

"They're better cold," I said.

We never planned to take up attending other people's funerals as a hobby, but once it started I think we both knew almost immediately what a boon to our relationship it was. It wasn't that things were going bad between the two of us, things were just *going* — going along in safe but unspectacular fashion, a lackluster walk down an uninspiring path that was leading to our own funerals somewhere down the line. There just didn't seem to be anything remarkable to *do* along the way.

We'd been married five years when we started, and up until then neither of us had shown any predilection for death. We are not necrophiles. I enjoy having sex with my very-alive wife, and I like to think she enjoys having it with me. And it's not the corpses that attracted us — not exclusively. We liked everything about funerals: the mourning, the sobbing, the eulogies, the buffets.

We stumbled upon our first funeral quite by accident. We were on our way to a wedding — Sylvia's boss's third marriage — and we were late and lost in some small town north of Montreal. I was driving and Sylvia was yelling at me to stop somewhere and ask for directions. I refused for as long as I could, and just when I had promised to stop at the next gas station, a church came into view. It was a stout white building with big red doors and a rather tall steeple. A white sandstone statue of Jesus stood on a marble pedestal out front, hands outstretched toward the street. Its parking lot, off to one side of the church, was full, and more parked cars lined the road.

"Quick, park," Sylvia demanded. She dreaded having to go to her boss's wedding almost as much as I did, but attendance, in an unwritten kind of way, was mandatory.

"Where?" I asked.

"Right there!" She pointed to a Kentucky Fried Chicken a little further down the road.

"They could tow us," I said.

"Do it quick and they won't notice."

I parked and we dashed hunched over through the parking lot, knuckles practically dragging on the pavement, imagining we were invisible. We laughed all the way to the road, then really picked up the pace. My dress shoes were tight and hurting me, but Sylvia was pulling me by the arm, just a little ahead of me. In her other hand she held her little black formal handbag, and she pressed that against her chest to keep from popping out of her top. She was wearing a light grey blazer, unbuttoned, with a darker grey, low-cut camisole underneath. Her skirt was simple and matched her hair: black, short and smart. She really looked stunning, even clodhopping in her heels, and I quite enjoyed the view from behind. I shook my arm free from her hand and gave her left buttock a quick squeeze. She swatted me backhandedly without stopping or turning around, and I heard her laugh. We bounded past the Jesus statue, stopped for a second to catch our breath in front of the red doors, and went inside arm in arm.

There was quiet, melancholic organ music playing, and I remember thinking it was pretty gloomy for a marriage. But I'd never been to anybody's third wedding and thought maybe it was normal. There were no ushers to greet us, but we were late. From what I'd seen of the church outside, the chapel was bigger than I expected. It was narrow, but long. There were at least forty pews of a dark, lacquered wood leading to the altar and all of them, save for the last three or four, were full. There was no bride in sight, which was a good sign; we weren't so late after all. A priest with a beard that made me think of Abe Lincoln was standing at the end of the centre aisle in front of the altar, and I scanned the area for the groom and his men.

I saw the coffin but Sylvia had me by the arm, and she pulled me into the third-to-last pew. She sat us near the middle, an older couple seated to her left. I was about to tell her we were in the wrong church, but she knelt in front of our seat before I had a chance to open my mouth. Sylvia is in no way a practicing Catholic, but the traditions of her childhood seem to take over when she finds herself inside a church. I waited patiently for her to finish praying, and exchanged a few stoical glances with the old man and woman beside us. Sylvia sat back up again, and she took hold of my hand in an automatic kind of way. I leaned over and whispered, "This isn't the right place. There's a casket up front." She craned her neck to look at the altar, and an expression of horror came over her face. I pulled gently at her hand and said as quietly as I could, "Let's get out of here."

I turned to my right and started to stand up, but more latecomers — six of them — shuffled into our pew. In the lead was an extremely fat woman wearing a baby blue dress that wrapped around her flabby body like a shawl. Even walking sideways, her stomach pressed hard against the back of the next pew and her rump scarcely squeezed by the bench behind. A man that I assumed was her husband, also plump but much taller, followed her, and behind him came four young and rotund girls. All six of them knelt in unison, and the woman snivelled hoarsely. Without looking up from his own prayer, the man put his arm around his wife's enormous shoulders, but his hand only made it to the centre of her neck. The organ music grew louder and more ominous. The fat family sat back in the pew, twelve hefty legs blocking our escape.

I motioned to Sylvia to go out the other way, past the elderly couple, and then the priest cleared his throat and began to speak. "Family and friends of Timothy Ellis, welcome." Sylvia wasn't moving, just staring ahead, her eyes on the priest. I nudged her gently toward our only viable exit route, but she resisted. The old man next to her was staring at me, I could feel his eyes but I avoided looking directly at him. I gave Sylvia another easygoing push.

She turned to me and whispered, rather loudly, "It's too late. Forget it."

I suppose normal people in our predicament would have quietly sat through the ceremony, slipped out as quickly and discreetly as possible afterwards, then dashed away to try and at least catch the end of the wedding we were supposed to attend. Maybe Sylvia and I aren't normal.

I must admit that I didn't pay much attention to the early stages of that first funeral. I stared at my shoes and tried to think of all the hockey games scheduled for that night. I've never placed a bet in my life, but I found myself making predictions — the mind can surprise at unexpected times. I remember pondering Buffalo and Vancouver — the Sabres were stronger but the Canucks were playing at home — when out of the corner of my eye I caught Sylvia putting a hand to her face. I turned slightly and saw her dabbing the skin beneath her eyes with the tips of her fingers. Her lips were puckered but parted, the expression she makes when she's holding back tears. Her eyes were trained on the front of the church. I nearly laughed but controlled myself.

I looked to the altar. There were five teenagers standing side by side, three girls and two boys, facing the congregation. Their heads were turned slightly to the left, however, looking up at the pulpit. Behind a wooden lectern and a thin microphone was another young woman, twenty years old at the most, with curly auburn hair, giving a eulogy. I tuned in.

"And sometimes I'd run into Pappy at the mall, where he used to go for coffee and to see his friends, and he'd be so proud to introduce me to them, even if he didn't remember that he'd already introduced me to them the week before." There was quiet, murmuring laughter in the church, followed by a few coughs. "Or the *day* before," she quipped with impeccable timing. This time the laughing was louder, I could hear it echoing, almost as if everyone had been simultaneously relieved of their grief, at least temporarily. I glanced at Sylvia. She put a hand over her mouth, laughed and coughed at the same time. "And he'd always tell them," the young woman continued, "this is my granddaughter Kelly. The one who plays hockey." Her voice broke over *hockey*, making her statement sound like a question. I could feel the congregation sniff collectively, seventy or more people all losing small pieces of their composure at once. "He was so proud of me," Pappy's granddaughter managed to whisper before backing away from the lectern. Everyone applauded. Sylvia was inconsolable.

By the end of the third or fourth grandchild speech, I was taken in as well. Pappy sounded like such a great guy. One of the kids, a skinny boy with an acne-ridden face, talked about how his grandfather used to call him "Stinky" and "Joe-Joe the Dog-Faced Boy" (I assumed the latter moniker was used before the onset of puberty actually did change his face for the worse). He said he knew it sounded kind of mean, taken out of context, but it used to make him laugh so much. The youngest looking girl read a poem she wrote in tribute to her grandfather, but she only made it through the first stanza and a bit of the second before breaking down. Kelly, the hockey player, stepped in and read the rest of the piece. There was a group "awww" spoken after each clever juvenile rhyme, and the last two lines touched me: "Now you're in a much better place/I hope you remembered to bring your violin case." Pappy had played the fiddle!

By the end of the ceremony, I felt like I had actually known Timothy Ellis — well enough to call him "Pappy," like his grandkids did. Sylvia was breathing deeply with that open pucker on her lips, a much-used ball of tissue crumpled in her hand. We stood up and I put my arm around her waist, hugging her a bit. Continuing on to the cemetery for the burial was automatic. We needed the closure.

Going to Pappy's house after the burial for tea and finger sandwiches with the rest of the mourners probably was not necessary for our emotional recovery, but we found ourselves following the procession of cars there nonetheless. It just seemed to cap the day off.

I passed myself off as the son of one of Pappy's old business associates (I heard someone say he'd been in textiles), and introduced Sylvia as my wife who had unfortunately never had the pleasure of meeting Mr. Ellis. I invented a tale of how Pappy had been very kind to my mother and myself when my own father passed away ten years before. I said that he came to comfort us the morning after my dad's sudden heart attack, and stayed and talked to my mom for over an hour. I told my story five or six times as Sylvia and I made the rounds of the room. Eventually I found the nerve to claim Pappy had played the violin at my father's funeral. That little addition went over big with his friends. We ate sandwiches and vegetables with dip. We drank tea and a little bit of white wine. After a while, desserts were laid out on a table. We had rum balls and millefeuilles.

Finally we drifted to the couches in the living room, where Pappy's immediate family had stationed themselves, allowing their friends to come to them. A long couch held four seated men, all in various stages of middle age. Some of the grandkids who had made speeches at the church milled about the room. An approximately forty-year-old woman stood with a plastic wine glass in her hand, the other resting on the back of a yellow easy chair. In the chair sat a very old and very frail looking woman. Blue-green oxygen tubes stuck out of her nostrils like big pliable straws, connected to a tank beside her on the floor. She had great folds of wrinkled skin furling out from under her eyes and chin, as if her bones had disintegrated and left her face rudderless. Brown age spots dotted her forehead, and her lips looked dry and crusty. In her shaky hands, also spotted like her forehead, she clutched a silver medal hanging from a green, red, and blue striped ribbon. One hand held the ribbon, the other the medal itself. I walked right up to her, escorting Sylvia on my arm, as if I'd known the woman for years.

"Mrs. Ellis," I said, reaching out with my hand. "My sympathies. I'm Spencer Fralick — my father was a colleague of Timothy's." The old woman freed one of her hands from the medal and touched my palm with her delicate fingers.

"This is my wife, Sylvia," I said, taking my hand back to point to her.

Sylvia crouched down in front of the easy chair and pulled the end of her skirt taut, edging it as close to her knees as she could. "Mrs. Ellis," she said, sweetly and softly. "It was such a beautiful service. Really."

One of the men pushed himself up off the couch and approached me. A single spiral of thin salt-and-pepper hair rested on his shiny forehead like a pig's tail. His face was similar to the old woman's, but he still had his bones. He thrust out a hand. "I'm Gregory Ellis."

I clasped his hand, it was sandpaper dry. "Spencer."

"Did I hear you say your father knew mine?" he asked.

"Yes," I answered quickly. For the first time all afternoon I felt nervous about my cover story. It was one thing to spin it to Pappy's friends and distant relatives, but here was one of his sons. With no other real choice, I plunged forward with it. "My father was Michael Fralick. He and your father knew each other from the business." I was proud of myself for calling it *the business* — it sounded so natural. "I can't tell you what a comfort your father was to my mother and I when my dad died. He was there the next morning, with donuts and milk, and he really consoled my mother."

"Fralick. Fralick," Gregory Ellis rolled my name over his tongue. "Funny, I don't remember that name."

I felt my stomach stagger, and the back of my neck got hot. I half-looked to Sylvia, hoping for a little assistance, but she was still hunkered down next to Pappy's widow, engrossed in conversation. The old lady was going on about the medal, the words *Battle of Hong Kong* in her wobbly voice. I gave my eyes back to Gregory Ellis. "Um," I began.

"But isn't that just like my dad?" he said cheerily. "He was always going off and doing things for people and never saying a word about it after. He was a humble man."

"Humble," I heard myself say, too relieved to be coherent.

Sylvia slipped her arm under the crook of my elbow. She introduced herself to Gregory Ellis, and then, to my surprise, said goodbye for the both of us. I didn't want to leave. After successfully pulling off my lie in front of the most challenging audience yet, I wanted to keep it going. I hadn't even mentioned the violin yet. But I had no choice except to go along with Sylvia; I was quickly learning that, on a team, one player must back up the other without hesitation. Sylvia squeezed my arm hard all the way to the door.

Outside, we paused on the front doorstep. I breathed the cool air and felt my body tingling all over. I don't think I realized how nervous I'd been — not just with Gregory Ellis, but with the whole situation, and all the tension and anxiety that had built up inside me was released at once, like a giant orgasm. I looked at Sylvia, and she, too, appeared to be in some kind of euphoric trance. Her eyes were half-crazed and half-dazed, and she looked beautiful, more so than ever before. We made off for the car together without speaking.

Beside me in the passenger seat, Sylvia bent her head toward her lap and stamped her feet repeatedly on the floor mat beneath them. She screamed; a deep, low howl that grew into a maniacal screech. I watched her, feeling the skin of my cheeks stretch as I smiled insanely. I let go and unleashed a shriek of my own. I turned the key in the ignition, revved the engine, and peeled out, the car squealing louder than the two of us put together.

"I . . . cannot . . . believe . . . what . . . we . . . just . . . did," I shouted, slapping the steering wheel once for each word. I bayed like a dog.

"That was insane!" Sylvia yelled back. "Totally in-fucking-sane!" The radio wasn't even on; it just seemed natural to speak as loudly as possible.

"I mean," I said, "What the FUCK did we just do? What . . . the . . . FUCK?" I slowed for a stop sign, cruised through it without stopping completely, and hit the gas again. It was getting dark fast, and there wasn't another pair of headlights in sight. Pappy had lived in a nice neighbourhood, lots of big houses with big yards that separated them. Sylvia snapped open her handbag, and thrust her hand inside. I checked the road. Then her hands were on the lapel of my suit jacket, pulling at it slightly. "What are you—?" I felt a distinct weight hanging from my lapel, not a lot, but enough to know something was there. I glanced down and saw the green, red, and blue ribbon and silver medal dangling from it.

"It's a souvenir," Sylvia said in a whisper. She sounded crazier than when she was screaming. "It's a trophy."

My first impulse was to stop the car, turn around, and return the stolen war medal. I was disgusted to have it pinned to my jacket — me, who had never so much as taken part in a fist fight, let alone a military battle. But Sylvia put both of her hands on my right thigh, kneaded it like dough, and my foot remained firmly planted on the gas pedal. "It's a trophy for you," she murmured seductively. I then gave in to my second impulse, pulled the car over and parked it beneath a heavy growth of overhanging willow branches. I turned off the ignition and killed the headlights.

We screwed violently in the front seat (for screwing is what it truly was; if you've screwed before you know the difference between that and "making love"; if you haven't I don't know what to tell you), and the aggression we let loose on each other felt like both punishment and reward for what we'd done. By the end of it, spent, with the side of my face squashed against the passenger window and Sylvia scrunched beneath me, I knew I deserved my trophy and wore it with pride.

I wish I could say that every subsequent visit we made to other people's funerals resulted in the unleashing of arousing emotions and carnal passion. We continued to have sex soon after, usually in the car on the way home, and it was good for the most part. But we just never seemed to attain the same level of fervour we felt that first time after Sylvia pinned Pappy's war medal on my jacket. She kept stealing little mementos from the funerals, too, and surprised me with them afterward. I hardly ever saw her doing it — she was too fast. We kept our souvenirs inside a cardboard box in a drawer in our kitchen; a tiny teddy bear, a couple of key rings, a Mont Blanc pen, and a handkerchief to name a few.

But none of these objects ever set a fire beneath us like the medal did, a fire built on both exhilaration and outrage. Without ever speaking about it out loud, I think we both hoped that Kyle Mather and his windshield wiper fluid might change that.

We spent a lot of time on wardrobe during the days leading up to what we had begun to call the Kyle Mather Long Weekend. He was to be shown on Thursday and Friday night at the Waxtall Parlour off Parc Avenue, followed by a funeral at St. Stephen's on Saturday morning. Sylvia said we needed new outfits for each day.

I had always hated shopping, but shopping for Kyle Mather's funeral was incredible. For the first time in my life I walked into stores actually looking for something nice to buy for myself. In the past I'd allowed Sylvia pick out my clothes, and I let her do it by herself because I despised the process of trying things on and finding them to be the wrong size or that they looked worse on me than on the rack. It made me feel self-conscious and humiliated in a small way. And looking for clothes for Sylvia was worse; it was always a lose-lose situation because if I said something looked nice on her but she didn't like it, she'd tell me I had no taste. And if I told her something didn't look nice on her she'd get all huffy and say I thought she was ugly. But shopping for three outfits each for the Kyle Mather Long Weekend was different; something overtook me, sort of in the same way that I get when I cook. I felt like I was creating art. I even found myself pointing out items for Sylvia to wear, and that really made her happy.

I wound up buying a conservative navy blue suit for the first viewing on Thursday, to go along with Sylvia's new, uncomplicated black long-sleeved dress. We both thought simply blending in with the crowd on the first night of the weekend extravaganza would be prudent. For the second night at the funeral home, I picked up a neat black outfit that was stylish, but at the same time appropriate for the occasion. No jacket, just a black long-sleeved shirt made of soft cotton that felt almost like velvet with a hem running down the middle that hid the buttons. A thin black tie, and stretchy but dressy black pants completed the ensemble. I could tell Sylvia was jealous of the way I was going to look on Friday night — she kept trying to convince me that it would be okay if she wore this short burgundy number with a floral pattern just slightly lighter than the rest of the skirt. I thought it showed too much thigh for the occasion (but added deftly that I quite enjoyed seeing it; I just didn't think the Mather family would). She said if she could find the right nylons, she could make it look right for a funeral home. I finally told her to go for it, as long as she promised to wear it for me some other time without the stockings.

We decided to go all out for our Saturday garbs, and it began to feel like we were getting married all over again. We laughed and joked over junky food-court meals, stole kisses on the escalators, and blithely put everything on the credit cards. And for a while, Kyle Mather was little more than an afterthought.

But the tragic tale of windshield wiper consumption was all over the news, and difficult to overlook. The stories had, by mid-week, evolved into endless exposés and investigative reports on underage drinking and the troubles parents encountered raising teens. The media was doing its utmost to evoke Kyle Mather's name at every possible opportunity; it was selling newspapers and drawing television viewers. It felt to Sylvia and me like our favourite indie band had suddenly been discovered by the masses, and the subsequent onslaught of hype was killing everything that was good about it before. I felt jealous when I heard about Kyle Mather on the radio, on TV. Sylvia complained nightly over dinner how everybody at her work was talking about him. We assured each other that nobody but us would dare to actually go to the funeral.

We were wrong.

On Thursday night we drove to the Waxtall Parlour in our first-night conservative outfits and had to park in a pay lot ten blocks away, the area was so inundated with cars. There was a considerable crowd hanging around outside the funeral home, none of them, I noted with scoff, dressed appropriately. Wrapping around the horde like a circus ring were a dozen television cameras, their bright white lights illuminating various patches of rubbernecks. Hand in hand, Sylvia and I pushed into the mass, edging our way around a television interview in-progress. A forty-something female subject, with her arm wrapped around the shoulders of a teenage girl, was telling the interviewer: "We just wanted to be here, first and foremost, to show our support and sympathy for the Mather family, and also to send a message to teens everywhere, including my own, that parents are ready and willing to talk." She took a deep breath, wiped her eyes, and gave her daughter a little squeeze. The teenager looked sullen and embarrassed. We shoved further into the crowd.

Adults our age and older stood about talking in groups. Many had their hands in the pockets of their shorts or jeans or Dockers. Others held Styrofoam cups from the Starbucks across the street against their protruding bellies. Some had placards with slogans like TEENS TALK PARENTS LISTEN printed on them. Teenagers gathered in clusters as well, many with their arms folded, looking like they didn't want to be there. I figured the friends of Kyle Mather, the mourning teens, were already inside. I pulled Sylvia toward the door, and saw a lineup of people on the nine or ten steps leading up to the funeral home. "We're never going to get in there," she said. I had to agree.

But our attire saved us. The people in line were dressed casually, like those in the crowd below. When Sylvia and I arrived at the bottom of the stairs, clad in my blue suit and her black dress, a gap in the line opened like magic. Parents and teens, unassociated with the Mathers but hopeful of getting inside, moved aside for us who, obviously to them, were either related to or close friends of the family. We donned our practiced mourning faces and thanked those who made room for us humbly. Within seconds we were whisked inside, the doors shut behind us by two white-gloved Waxtall attendees.

It was very posh inside the building; Waxtall Parlour was of a slightly higher class than Sylvia and I were used to. There was no paint on the walls, just natural, light brown wood. An impressive-looking reception desk sat in one corner of the lobby, and next to it a huge rectangular fish aquarium. A big Betta Splender with a green, blue and gold body and fluttery red fins swam slowly and regally. A dozen tiny goldfish darted around beside it, under it, above it, accentuating the Betta's unperturbed magnificence. The carpeting was slightly industrial, but a nice, soft beige. There was even a kids' playroom at the far end of the long front hall, where young children could occupy themselves and stay out of the adults' way. I was very impressed, and the look of things made up slightly for the annoying crowd outside.

But it was difficult to move, even in the lobby, the place was so packed. I found myself sucking in my stomach and holding my arms close to my sides to try and maneuver around in the throng. Teenagers were everywhere, grimy streaks of dried tears accentuating their pimples. The adults seemed to be either on the verge or at the end of crying. Sylvia rested her head against my chest for a moment; to everyone it looked like she had walked in and was immediately overcome with grief. I, too, believed that to be the case at first, but then I glanced down and saw she was stealthily smearing her mascara with the tips of her fingers. I wondered why she felt she needed to do this, the funeral home usually brought out her emotions, smeared makeup and all, naturally. I thought maybe she was nervous — this was a big event — but it wasn't the time to start asking. We had a body to view.

Snug inside an open mahogany casket, inert hands folded across the third and fourth buttons of his best suit jacket, Kyle Mather seemed utterly at peace, completely serene. He looked a little different from the photos that ran in the papers all week, but I had to admit the mortician had performed magnificent work. Kyle looked as if he had simply died quietly in his sleep, in the middle of a very nice dream. Gazing upon his corpse, I forgot for a moment about the windshield wiper fluid he had drunk behind the high-school gymnasium just one week before. I found myself looking forward to a first-class weekend, despite the lurkers outside.

Standing off to the side of the casket were Kyle's parents, whom I recognized from all the news stories on television. They were a nice-looking couple, about ten years older than Sylvia and I. Christopher Mather was medium in height, thin of frame and hair, and wore a navy suit much like my own. His wife Michelle was very short, I'm not even sure she was five feet tall, kind of round, with curly blond hair pinned tightly around her head. She wore a simple black dress that made her look dignified. She really seemed to be keeping it together, and I marvelled at her bravery. They were both putting on brave faces, in fact, as an impromptu condolence line had formed from the casket to where they stood. They met each person with handshakes, embraces, or both, and sometimes a little smile broke out on their faces.

I hadn't spent nearly as much time as I would have liked to in front of the casket before Sylvia and I were edged aside by the inertia of the crowd, and we found ourselves in the middle of the condolence line. I looked at Sylvia and motioned with my eyes toward the far end of the room, silently asking her if she wanted to slip out of line. We had been so busy preparing our outward appearances for the event that we hadn't taken the time to agree on a cover story. Sylvia shook her head no, and turned to peer around the man in front of her in line, trying to see and hear the Mathers. I was a little miffed, so I decided that if Sylvia wanted to plunge right in I'd let her do all the talking. Also annoying was an older woman who had taken a place in line behind me. She, too, was trying to get a view of Kyle's parents, and she kept leaning against me and stepping on the backs of my shoes to do it. I stayed still, not moving to accommodate her, and steamed silently.

The line seemed painfully slow, but moved gradually. Soon I could overhear the little conversations taking place at the front. Lots of standard commiseration, but the Mathers seemed to know everyone, called them all by name. This raised my irritation, and Pushy Woman behind me wasn't helping matters. My ears perked up, however, when I heard Mr. Mather start to talk to a man about a special family heirloom of some kind. He removed something from his breast pocket and held it out in his palm for the man to see. It was an old-fashioned gold watch; the round kind with a cover that has to be lifted to see the face. It had a thin, delicate chain hanging from it. Mr. Mather lifted the watch higher and held it to the man's ear, who nodded with an impressed look on his face. I saw Sylvia had picked up on the conversation as well; she was leaning in as close as she could.

It was difficult for Mr. Mather to get the words out, he was overcome for a moment, but I heard him explain that the watch had been his father's, and his grandfather's before that. It in fact went back two more generations, and a tradition among the Mathers existed where, over the years, the watch was passed from father to eldest son. Mr. Mather's friend wiped an eye at this news. It was obvious from his reaction that Kyle had been the Mathers' only child. "What will you do with it?" the man asked sombrely. Sylvia reached her hand back and patted me repeatedly on the arm.

Mr. Mather tried to answer, but the words wouldn't come out. His wife put her arm around his waist, and said just above a whisper, "It will go with Kyle."

Sylvia turned around to face me, took both of my hands in hers and gave me a sneaky smile. Her eyes were wide and crazed. I knew she wanted the watch, wanted it bad. I got a sick feeling in my stomach. I looked at her sternly and shook my head no. Taking little souvenirs was fine and even exciting, but a watch that had been handed down through the generations with no generation left to be handed down to, a watch destined to be buried with Kyle Mather, was too much for me. "Don't do it," I whispered. "Not that." Sylvia's cheeks went red and her brow crumpled, her eyes became slits, aimed angrily at my own. She squeezed my hands hard, so hard that I yanked them free. In doing so, I elbowed Pushy Woman in the stomach by accident.

Pushy Woman yelped like an injured dog and staggered around, holding her midsection. I reached out, one arm in front of her, one behind, in case she fell. The condolence line broke up and became completely disorganized as other people came to her aid. Pushy Woman's eyes and mouth opened wide as she gasped for breath. Her knees buckled and she collapsed into my arms. Somebody cried out, "Mrs. Werdmuller's having a heart attack! Call 911! Call 911!" Three Waxtall attendees came running into the room with their white gloves on. Bodies circulated around me like an assembly line of pop bottles gone mad. Still supporting Pushy Woman, I glanced around to see where Sylvia was. My throat burned when I finally saw her.

Christopher Mather was at the edge of the crowd surrounding Pushy Woman and me, looking on with his wife beside him. Sylvia stood right behind them. Then she turned sideways and slipped between them, pardoning herself with a smile, her hands just barely touching Christopher's suit jacket. He paid Sylvia no heed, kept his eyes on Pushy Woman.

Two of the Waxtall attendees relieved me of Pushy Woman — Mrs. Werdmuller — and eased her into a chair the third had brought over. I slipped away, looking for my wife. She was escorting the Mathers to some chairs in the back of the room. I marched in their direction, hoping I wasn't already too late to stop her. If she thought she was going to pilfer the Mather family watch, she was gravely mistaken.

Sylvia got Christopher and Michelle Mather to sit down in side-by-side chairs, and started fawning over them. She heard me approach, and turned around with a bright — too bright — look on her face.

"Honey! Just in time!" She turned to the Mathers, "Folks, this is my husband, Spencer."

Christopher Mather began to rise, but I gracefully motioned him back into his seat and shook his hand in one fluid motion. Michelle's hand I took in both of mine and gave it a reassuring squeeze.

"Dear, Mrs. Mather could use a drink of water. Be a dear and get her some?" Sylvia said in a really exaggerated sweet voice. The "dears" and "honeys" really bugged me, it was so fake.

Christopher Mather stood up. "Thank you but it's really not necessary," he said, "I can go." He straightened his jacket. Then he patted the left side of his chest. A look of panic came over his face and he thrust his hands into all the pockets of his jacket and pants. He wheeled and looked at the empty chair where he'd been sitting. He turned to his wife. "The watch. Do you have it?"

Michelle Mather looked shocked. Christopher started retracing his steps to the casket, his head down, darting back and forth as he scanned the floor. His wife began to weep, still sitting in the chair, seeming unable to move. Sylvia crouched in front of her. "Don't worry," she said in an encouraging voice, "I'm sure it'll turn up. It's got to be around her somewhere." She turned to me. "Please. *Honey*. Go get Mrs. Mather some water."

I took off in search of refreshment for the mother of the deceased. I had no choice now except to perform my duty as one of the two players on our team. Anything else would have raised suspicions. Sylvia had the watch, I knew, and I had been too late to stop her. I didn't want her to have it, but I also didn't want her to get into trouble for having it. And I'd thought of a way for her to give it back without anybody knowing she'd stolen it in the first place. There was still time.

On my way out of the room I passed Mrs. Werdmuller in her chair, fanning her face with her hand before a gathered group of the concerned. She seemed to be breathing normally. It occurred to me that the one person forgotten in all the commotion was Kyle Mather himself. He lay unattended in his coffin, and I had a wonderful opportunity to get a really good look, but I was no longer in the mood. It was all getting to me — the crowd of gawking jerks outside, the television cameras, the impossibility to move inside and, most of all, Sylvia. I wished we had never come. I felt like a hypocrite for being mad at her for taking the watch. Except for that brief moment of disgust I experienced after she stole Pappy Ellis's war medal, I had been nothing except enthusiastic about her thievery. Finding out what she'd taken from funerals was always so exciting — for both of us. But from our brief exchange just before I accidentally elbowed Mrs. Werdmuller she knew I was against robbing the Mather family watch. She had crossed a line that I, at least, could see clearly.

There was a cafeteria in the basement of the Waxtall Parlour, and I went downstairs to get some water. It was pretty full down there, too, lots of people lounging around eating donuts and drinking coffee. The cigarette smoke was thick in the air. Under normal circumstances I would have run back up to tell Sylvia about the dessert spread and the big coffee percolator, but my heart wasn't in it anymore. I grabbed a little bottle of spring water and left the Danishes for the real mourners.

When I got back upstairs Sylvia was deep in conversation with the man that Mr. Mather had shown the watch to just before all the commotion started. They both shook their heads solemnly, synchronized expressions of astonishment that the watch was missing. Michelle Mather had joined her husband in the search, along with some of the mourners and a few Waxtall attendees. I walked up to Sylvia and took her hand. "Excuse us," I said politely to the man, "maybe we can help find it." I pulled my wife gently but firmly away.

I guided her to the back wall and started walking around the perimeter of the room, pretending to look for the watch on the ground. "Here's the water," I gestured with the bottle. "You want to give it to her?"

"Later."

"Don't you have something else you want to give her?"

"Spencer, shut up," she snapped in a whisper. She bent down to look under a chair, putting on a real show.

"You can pretend you found it. Give it back."

"I won't," she said, standing up. "Shut up about it. People will hear you."

"Sylvia, I don't want you to do this. It's wrong."

She walked away from me quickly and headed straight for a row of chairs lined against another wall. She began checking under each of them. I stuffed the water bottle in my inside jacket pocket and jogged to catch up with her.

She took a seat near the end of the row of chairs, right next to an elderly woman resting her forearms on a wooden cane. Sylvia looked at me approaching and gave me a big smile, like she didn't know I had been right behind her the whole time. "Spencer," she sang, extending her left arm, "come and sit." I did, and she kept me there for the next half-hour, protected from me by the lady with the cane.

In the car she tried to be seductive about the watch. She took it out from inside her bra and dangled it between two fingers for me to see. I told her I didn't want to look at it, that it made me sick to even think about it. She was patient, though, and persistent, and she started rubbing my right knee and thigh. "Come on, Spencer, look. It's beautiful."

I shoved her hand away. "Leave me alone. I'm trying to drive."

"Come on Spence, this is the best thing we ever got!"

"We?" I said angrily. "We? Sorry, darlin'. There's only one person who stole the watch and it's you. They were going to bury it with that kid. Sylvia, you're sick."

She put her hand on my leg again, this time higher up on my thigh. I tried to push her away but she persisted. "Spencer," she meowed, "why don't you pull over somewhere nice and quiet?"

"Forget it."

"Spencer?" she said softly, alluringly. I felt her hand on my crotch. For a moment I considered giving in to her, if only for the immediate reward. But as I grew hard I felt repulsed. I swatted her hand. "Ow!" she cried, recoiling to her seat.

"What's the matter with you?" I said. "How could you? How could you even consider taking their watch?"

She let me have it then. "What's the matter with *me*? You're the one with the problem. One day you love it and the next you're all high and mighty about it. You have to decide Spencer, if you're into this or not."

"I'm into it, just not for the watch."

"No — you see — it can't be like that. You have to either be in or out. You can't pick and choose. I'm the one sticking my neck out. You can't all of the sudden tell me you don't like what I'm taking. I decide what to take."

"Now you're just making up rules."

"What?"

"You're making up rules, Sylvia, to suit yourself. Just like with everything — whatever suits you is fine for both of us. I'm sick of it."

Sylvia slumped in her seat and said nothing. We were driving over the Mountain to get back home, on the street snootily named The Boulevard that snakes through part of the residential section of Westmount. I imagined there were more watches like the Mathers' inside many of the obscenely large houses in the neighbourhood.

"I never wanted to go to these funeral things in the first place," I continued, lying. "I was just doing it to please you. To keep the peace." I reached into my jacket pocket and took the water bottle out. "You see," I snapped, brandishing the water, "now you've got *me* stealing stuff, too. I don't want to have anything to do with it." I rolled down my window and threw the bottle out.

Before I had a chance to roll the window back up, Sylvia's unbuckled her seatbelt and leaned across my body. I cocked my head to the side to see the road in front of me and told her to sit down before she got us both killed. She whispered, "Asshole," and threw something out the window before recoiling back to her seat.

I knew she'd dumped the watch, and I slammed on the brakes. Horns blasted from behind and one car swerved around my left. I edged over to the curb slowly, and switched on the hazards. I got out of the car and made my way across the street, stopping to let cars pass and running when I had the chance. When I reached the other side I looked back and Sylvia was in the driver's seat of our car, putting it into gear. With indifference I watched her speed off, abandoning me. Somehow, I was just not surprised.

I scoured the side of the road for what seemed like an hour. I felt as if finding the watch would make me the winner of the argument, and would make Sylvia feel really guilty about taking off on me. As I searched, I went through lots of different coming-home scenarios in my mind. I rehearsed a silent, passive-aggressive approach, one in which I'd walk into the house and without saying a word, hand the watch to Sylvia, and then go out again and stay in a motel for the night by myself. I considered an irate entrance, with screaming and yelling and scolding, and telling Sylvia we were going back the next night to give the watch back, that I'd do it by myself if I had to. I half-wished I'd get hit by a car, so Sylvia would have to come to the hospital with the knowledge that she'd put me there.

The watch wasn't anywhere, and I was tired of looking for it. I was also starting to get scared the people in the neighbourhood might notice me snooping around, take me for a prowler and call the police. I decided to hail the next cab that happened by and just go home and try to forget about the whole thing. And then I kicked the watch. I had probably been over the patch of grass where it lay ten or eleven times, but only after giving up did I come upon it by mistake. That's what this whole other people's funerals thing was, I told myself, a mistake.

Sylvia was lying on the couch in the living room with the lights out and the TV on when I walked in. I stood for a moment to the side of the couch, waiting for her to speak first. But she didn't say anything, didn't even look over at me. I took the watch from my jacket pocket and held it out in my palm. "Well. I found it." Sylvia grunted quietly, eyes glued to the television. I tossed the watch in the air, underhanded, and she caught it without turning her head. "I *said*, I found it!" Sylvia looked at it unceremoniously, turned it over in her hands like she was inspecting a dirty dish. She then rose and sulked upstairs to our bedroom, taking the watch with her. I turned the television off and hung my suit over a chair in the living room. I lay down on the couch in my boxers and undershirt and tried to sleep.

At first I was completely steamed up, still too angry to imagine ever speaking to my wife again. I actually fantasized a little about never ever opening my mouth to say another word. I'd still live in the house, though, just to torture Sylvia for the rest of her life. After a few minutes of that I started to feel bad, so I settled on silence for a week, which eventually became five days, three days, and then just until the next night. I started wishing Sylvia would just come downstairs and make up with me. I could have gone upstairs myself, but she was the one who took off with the car, she was the one who stranded me in Westmount. Still, with each passing hour I wished harder and harder that we were simply over this.

I woke up and the clock on the VCR glowed a green 4:56. I didn't remember dozing off. Nearly the entire night had passed and no Sylvia. All the rage I had worked myself down from returned. A plan formed in my mind, revenge its end result.

I wore what I'd planned to wear on Saturday to the Friday night viewing; I didn't intend on attending the funeral itself anymore. It was a dark suit with a three-quarter jacket and a royal blue shirt. The tie was dark, too, with a few hints of gold. I felt like Johnny Cash.

It seemed everybody at the funeral parlour was talking about the missing watch. "Terrible," "unthinkable," and "heartless" were the words I most often heard to describe the thievery in conversations around me. I tried to ignore it, tried to sell myself the notion that it was Sylvia's doing, alone, not mine. I mainly hung out in the basement with the food. I ate my fill three, maybe four, times over. I could tell people were looking at me and whispering about what I pig I was making of myself. I paid my detractors no heed and shovelled more potato salad onto my Styrofoam plate. I finished off the coffee in the percolator with my fifth cup and demanded one of the white-gloved Waxtall attendees make more. I felt drunk in my belligerence, and probably looked it, but I hadn't touched a drop. I didn't know if Sylvia had dared show up or not — she certainly hadn't come down to the cafeteria — but I had more pressing matters on my mind. Getting to my hiding place was the first on my list.

I left the basement at quarter to ten, fifteen minutes before the end of the viewing. I made my way casually down the long hall, passing people walking in the opposite direction, on their way out. I went by the room where Kyle

Mather's body lay and, even though I tried not to, looked in to see if Sylvia was there. The room was pretty stark. Christopher and Michelle Mather still held court near the casket, but only eight or nine people were waiting around to say goodbye. Sylvia was not among them, but I wasn't really surprised. She already had what she wanted.

I continued down the hall and stopped when I came to the kiddie room. It was separated from the hall by a glass partition, so the entire room was visible. In one corner of the playroom was a television with one of the *Lion King* movies playing on the screen. There were four big, soft-looking cushions set up in front of the TV — red, green, blue, and orange, but they were empty. The whole room was deserted, in fact. I guessed *The Lion King* played over and over, whether anybody watched or not. All around the perimeter were toys; plastic trucks and wooden blocks, a child-sized play kitchen with miniature pots, pans, and a kettle, a chalkboard with drawings of trees and houses and people on it, an orange tractor with black plastic wheels that a four-year-old might ride. And dominating the centre of the room, encased in clear plexiglas, was the ball pit. Red balls, blue balls, yellow balls, green balls. I'd always thought the ball pit was nothing more than a kiddie cage; a giant cubbyhole to stow children in whenever taking care of them became inconvenient. At that moment, the ball pit was one of the most convenient things I'd ever come across.

The squeeze through the circular entrance to the pit was a little tight, but I managed. My landing was soft, especially thanks to the fact that my arms reached the floor of the pit beneath the balls while my body was still halfway through the entrance, and therefore eased my fall. Once in, I immediately turned over onto my back and started burying myself in the balls. I swayed my hips to dig down and used my arms to gather balls and place them on top of my body. I had never been in a ball pit before — I think I was eighteen or nineteen the first time I saw one — and I'd always harboured a secret desire to try one out. I never thought I'd get a chance, but there I was, completely covered in balls, with just a little space around my nose and mouth exposed. It was surprisingly ergonomic in the pit; the balls provided both lumbar and lower back support of a quality I had never experienced. I couldn't help but roll back and forth a bit, enjoying the feeling of balls revolving soothingly against my back. Soon I made myself stay still, however. The pit was, after all, supposed to be my hiding place.

After about an hour of lying among the balls I heard singing from far off. It grew closer, a really bad, off-key male voice mangling the words to "Where the Streets Have No Name" by U2. I smelled cigarette smoke. I didn't dare sit up to look but I knew whoever was there was right in the kiddie room with me. I tried not to breathe. The singing stopped and there was silence for a moment, save for the never-ending *Lion King* voices on the television. There was a big bang on the plexiglas surrounding the ball pit and I convulsed once in fear. A few balls rolled around on top of me. Another bang. I turned my eyes to the right but didn't see anything. Then a series of bangs, like bongo drumming. I turned my eyes to the left and saw one of the Waxtall attendees, college-aged, white gloves removed, a cigarette hooked in the corner of his mouth, eyes closed, head shaking to his own private beat on the plexiglas. I remained as still as I could. The kid thankfully put an end to the drum solo after about a minute. Then I heard the *Lion King* voices go away. The lights went out in the kiddie room and I felt safe again.

It was boring after that, but I endured what I judged to be two more hours of lying as still as possible. My resolve to hurt Sylvia kept me focused. Finally, I decided to take a chance at looking at my watch and sat up in the ball pit. My joints were pretty stiff and my back didn't feel as good as it had when I first got inside. It was almost pitch black in the place, only a few strips of white light lay across various parts of the kiddie room thanks to the street lamps outside. I checked the time, using the little green light on my watch. It was just after one. I slipped a slim cat burglar flashlight out of my inside jacket pocket and used it to find the opening in the pit plexiglas. I slid out and into the hallway.

It was only then that I started to get the creeps. My encounter with the amateur musician in the kiddie room had put a scare in me, but this was different. Being alone — and especially *feeling* alone — out in the hallway was eerie. Armed with only the narrowly focused light of my flashlight, I started to think unreasonably about how if the dead in the funeral home suddenly got up and walked and decided to take revenge on behalf of all the dead I'd disrespected in visiting other people's funerals, there'd be no one to save me. I tried hard to keep my mind on my job, my plan, and continued down the hall.

In the basement, there were two closed doors down the hall and around a corner from the cafeteria. I found the door handle to the first one with my flashlight. I was surprised and happy it was unlocked. Inside it was completely dark, and I could hear a slow but steady pinging from within. I remained at the edge of the doorway and aimed my flashlight beam in the sound's direction, illuminated an industrial spray faucet hanging above a deep stainless steel sink installed in the back wall. I reached around the doorframe with my right arm and patted the wall with my palm, feeling for a light switch. When the whole room came into view I gagged and coughed, trying to keep the potato salad down, and turned my eyes out into the dark hall while I felt for the light switch once again. I only got a look for a couple seconds, but I knew I wouldn't find Kyle's body there; I knew he'd already passed through this room. It almost was all white and silver; white walls and white floors, silver sinks, tables, trays, and equipment. Some long and thin yellow tubes whose purpose I didn't like thinking about, though it wasn't hard to guess. A scent of sterilization, a combination of Ajax and Windex. But what made me look away so quickly was a motionless figure lying on a stainless steel table in the middle of the room, a naked old man, skin white like typing paper. I shut the door, glad to feel the plush softness of the carpet beneath my feet in the hallway.

I found the coffins in the second room across from the cafeteria. I located Kyle's mahogany casket with my flashlight and approached it warily, still a little spooked from the other room. I steeled myself against my natural, instinctive terror and opened the lid.

A hundred cold pin needles poked the back of my neck and shoulders, and I quivered with a chill. I tried hard not to look directly at Kyle's corpse, told myself to just get the job done, but appropriately enough, morbid curiosity took over. I shone my light in his face and wondered what separated me from a guy like Kyle Mather. I used to drink a lot, too, when I was in high school — how come I never mistook motor oil for Jack Daniels or liquid bleach for vodka? How drunk do you have to get before you don't notice you're drinking windshield wiper fluid? I thought about how the papers said Kyle only died three days after ingesting the fluid. At first they thought he was simply sick with alcohol poisoning; not the most benign self-induced ailment but one most people managed to recover from. But he never got better, just worse. By the time they figured out what was really wrong the poison had already spread, carried by his own bloodstream, to all of his organs and his brain. I stared up the dead boy's nostrils, counted his nose hairs, and thought about how stupid a way to go this was. And how Kyle Mather's stupidity was ruining my marriage.

I slipped the flashlight between my teeth to see by and stuffed both of my hands into my left and right jacket pockets. I emptied them, two items at a time, on top of Kyle's formaldehyde-filled and rigor-sturdy chest. The handkerchief, the Mont Blanc pen, the miniature teddy bear, all the key rings, the postcard from Albuquerque with the 1960 postmark, the Girl Guide Bookbinding merit badge, the green golf ball, the Boba Fett action figure, and finally, Pappy's war medal; everything from our drawer of treasured funeral souvenirs. The Mather family may have lost their cherished family watch, and I was truly sorry for that, but their son would be buried with mementos from nearly ten other families. And best of all, they would be lost forever to Sylvia.

I started hiding the stuff in various parts of the casket. The flatter objects I slid into the small space between the inner coffin wall and the cushion Kyle's body lay on. Others I slipped under his back. I got a notion to pin Pappy's medal on the dead kid's jacket, but I knew that even if the funeral the next day wasn't open casket his parents were sure to take one last look. I placed it under the cushion beneath his head instead.

There was a noise, creeping footsteps out in the hall. I killed the flashlight and closed the casket lid as quickly as my suddenly numb fingers allowed. I felt my way carefully to the corner of the room abreast of the door and crouched down against the wall beside some kind of a table or counter. I heard the door handle turn and a flashlight beam danced into the room. My heart was racing and I felt cold in the back of my neck and head. I tried to mask my breathing by inhaling and exhaling in extremely slow, deliberate succession. I felt like I was suffocating.

The flashlight beam danced about the room, as if searching. I tried to make myself as small as possible, curled in my ball in the corner. I couldn't see who was holding the flashlight; it was pitch black everywhere except where the light happened to shine at any one moment. It caught the side of Kyle's casket and remained fixed there. The round light beam on the mahogany wood grew continuously smaller and soon I could see feet — a pair of women's shoes, black — in the outer edges of the light's radiance, walking toward the casket. As she drew nearer, more and more of her became illuminated. Bare calves, bony knees, a flash of thigh, and the hem of a burgundy skirt decorated with flowers.

"I thought you were going to wear nylons with that dress," I intoned dryly. Sylvia yelped and dropped her flashlight on the floor.

I stood up and turned my flashlight on my wife's face. "What the hell are you doing here?"

"Spencer?" She shielded her eyes from the glow, looking frightened. "Is that you?"

"Yeah it's me. What do you think you're doing?" I was scared Sylvia had come to raise her obsession with the dead to the next, unthinkable, level.

"Get that light out of my eyes," she whispered. "You're scaring me."

I pointed my flashlight up at the ceiling and approached her. She rushed forward and attacked me with a strong, clinging hug, the side of her face flat against the front of my shoulder. I was still angry but out of a sense of duty stroked the back of her head with my palm. "Sylvia, what are you doing here?"

She broke her embrace and stood up straight. She reached down the front of her dress, dug into the left cup of her bra, and pulled out the watch. "I came to put it back."

I reached for my wife's waist and hugged her hard against my body. I pressed my forehead to her shoulder. "Sylvia, I'm sorry. I'm really sorry." She patted me on the back, but very softly, as if she didn't know why she needed to comfort me.

"It's okay," she said into my ear. "I'm the one that should be sorry." She straightened out her arms and looked me in the eyes. "I want to give it back. And I want to give back the other things."

"They're here," I said, sniffing.

"Who?"

"Not who — what. The medal, everything. They're here."

"Where?"

I pointed my flashlight at Kyle's casket. She went over to it and lifted the lid. I joined her and put my arm around her shoulder. We stared at the teenager's body together and, for a moment, it felt like I was looking upon our own child, though I knew all too well we'd never have one. I think Sylvia felt the same way, and we both had a little cry.

I slid my hand under the cushion and pulled out Pappy's war medal, handed it to Sylvia. She took it, one last look, and put it right back where it had been. Then she placed the Mather family watch on Kyle's chest. She reached for the lid. I helped her ease it closed.

The glaring flaw in my plan was its ending. In my mind, slipping the mementos into Kyle's coffin *was* the end, but it was only after completing this that I realized I had neglected to work out a safe way of getting out of the funeral parlour. To my disappointment, neither had Sylvia. We decided on the simplest and most direct route and took our chances with the front door.

It became apparent this was not the quietest way to leave as soon as we unlocked the door from the inside. The parlour's alarm system blared in our ears as we dashed down the front steps. We ran through the front courtyard area, where the crowds and television cameras had gathered the night before, and cut onto the sidewalk. Sylvia was lagging behind a bit so I reached back and grabbed her arm, pulling her in the direction of our car. Police sirens wailed in the distance, and the red, white, and blue flashing lights of a cruiser appeared as it turned the corner three blocks in front of us. I could see the lights of another coming straight down the road behind it. I stopped running and hooked Sylvia's arm under mine.

The first police car sped past us, continued on toward the Waxtall Parlour. The second car slowed and stopped when it came abreast of Sylvia and me. My heart was racing and my legs went weak. Drops of sweat slipped down my flanks but my teeth were chattering. There were two police officers in the car, a woman behind the wheel and a man in the passenger seat who shone a bright light over Sylvia and me. My knees buckled. Sylvia kept me from falling.

"Everything okay?" the policeman asked in French.

I stammered something incomprehensible in reply. I had little strength in my legs and leaned heavily against Sylvia for support. The officer opened his door and put one foot on the pavement of the road.

"Everything's fine, thank you," I heard Sylvia say. "I'm just *trying* to get my husband to the car. It's my fault, really. He didn't want to go to my office party in the first place, so, really, can I blame him for getting so drunk?"

My body was temporarily incapacitated but my mind was working quite well. Well enough to be in awe of yet another skill my wife possessed that, like pickpocketing, I had been unaware of before: the art of improvisation.

"And you," the policeman asked Sylvia, "you're okay to drive?"

"Of course. I never touch a drop. But thank you for asking. You know, it's really nice to know the police are concerned enough to stop and see if people need help. Lots of people think the police don't care, but clearly—"

"Well, have a good night," the officer interrupted, his eyes on the road ahead. He closed his door, raised his eyebrows, and gave his partner a wry look. "Safe drive," he said, turning back to us. The car sped off to join the other at the funeral parlour.

Though I felt better almost immediately after the police were gone, I allowed Sylvia to continue supporting me as I pointed out where I'd parked our car. She opened the passenger door for me and I got in. When Sylvia started the car we both sighed hugely. She laid her hand gently on my left thigh, let out another sigh, and patted my knee three times. She put the car in gear and made off for home.

Once there, we didn't speak, just held hands and walked silently into the house together. Sylvia went upstairs and I went into the kitchen. I poured two short glasses of brandy and carried them up to our room. Sylvia was waiting on the bed, still dressed in her burgundy outfit. She took her brandy and drank half of it, put the glass on the bedside table. I drank half of mine and sat down on the bed.

We had just pulled off the most daring and dangerous ruse in our short other people's funerals careers. But we celebrated slowly. Tenderly. We made love until the pink light of morning edged its way through our bedroom window. We fell asleep to the sound of singing birds and the neighbourhood recycling collection truck's motor.

We don't go to other people's funerals anymore. It's out of our systems. We've joined a Monday night line-dancing group and a club that meets once a month to discuss novels that have been adapted as Hollywood movies. And we've tried snowshoes for the first time. Anything to make that march down the path to our respective funerals more interesting.

BLOAT

It had gotten so bad that Geoff couldn't do anything without a stomach full of pasta, burgers, pizza — anything. And once he'd eaten enough to get himself into a state where he could actually do something, the will and the energy would come in quick, short bursts that invariably crashed after ten, fifteen minutes. Then he'd lie on the floor and roll around holding his stomach, heart hammering as his body worked at digesting, the bloated feeling risen all the way up to his throat. If he wasn't such a chickenshit he'd plunge two fingers back there and puke it up. Instead he just lay around, waiting for his body to break down the food and send it to other places besides his gullet. After a while a hint of relief would come, his stomach just a little less full, eventually emptier with time, until finally there was nothing left and the need to do it all over again came to him like the need to come up for air from the bottom of a lake.

Geoff liked Tatiana — a lot. He wrote her letters he never sent, but it was hard work. A big bag of Doritos, a few snack cakes, and a two-litre bottle of Pepsi meant three, maybe four paragraphs. Rolling around on the floor, the cola sloshing around audibly in his stomach, he'd think about the next declaration in his manifesto of love. Sometimes he'd forget what he wanted to say by the time he'd eaten himself up to where he could write again.

Tatiana smoked Dutch cigarettes and wore green a lot. Bright greens that reminded Geoff of the green crayon that came in the box he had as a kid marked "NEW! NEONS." Yesterday he devoured twenty-four fish sticks and worked up the guts to ask her how she got a name like Tatiana — she didn't have an accent and her hairstyle was contemporary.

"My parents liked Russian stuff," she said, wrapping a napkin around his ice cream cone, three teetering scoops: chocolate chocolate chip, mint chocolate chip, and orange. "I have a sister, you know." She leaned her elbows up on the counter and handed him the cone. "She's younger. Her name's Kelly. I guess they got over the Russian thing. That's two seventy-five."

Geoff paid and turned to leave. Tatiana called after him. "Wait up. I'm going on break." He said he couldn't wait.

When he got home he boiled water in the biggest pot he had. He made the whole bag of rigatoni. He had no sauce in his apartment, but made do with butter, parmesan cheese, and paprika. He ate sitting on his living room couch, right out of the pot, a dishtowel on his lap to keep from burning himself. He thought about what might have been had he stayed for Tatiana's break. He imagined himself on the ice cream parlour terrace, at one of the wooden picnic tables, licking his cone, Tatiana across the bench from him, smoking, her white, chocolate-stained apron in a ball on the table, her blond hair tied back tight in a ponytail, work-style, the hairnet still on, like she didn't notice it anymore. The features of her face were small, delicate. Three little freckles under her left eye, two under her right. What would they talk about? Robertson Davies books, Geoff decided. He'd better get reading.

But the other fantasy was more appealing. He pictured a small room with no furniture or windows. The floor would be all covered in Pizza Hut pizzas, laid out in neat rows like checkers on a board, all the varieties, all the different types of crusts. Tatiana waiting for him in the middle of the room, lying on the floor, on the pizza, dressed in a neon green miniskirt and tank top, nibbling on a stalk of celery. Bare feet, toes stuck inside the crusts of two Stuffed Crust Veggie Lovers. She raises one leg in the air to wave to him and the yellow-white cheese stretches between her toes and the floor, expanding tighter and thinner until it snaps, recoils into a melted stringy ball. He steps inside the room, steps right on a Twisted Crust pepperoni and cheese. He's not wearing shoes. He's not wearing anything. She can see how fat he is so he dives head-first before she has time for a really good look, slides easily on the pizzas, like sliding on ice, and comes to rest at Tatiana's feet. Propped up on one elbow, he places a mushroom between her big toe and second toe, a slice of pepperoni between the next two, a green pepper between the next, and a hunk of cheese between the last. An all-dressed foot shish kabob. He opens his mouth.

After swallowing the last bite of rigatoni, Geoff whisked two fingers around the bottom of the pot, scooped butter, parmesan, and paprika into his mouth. He felt energized, got out his notebook full of letters and began to write.

"Dear Tatiana. I'm sorry for blowing you off when you asked me to stay for your break. I guess I was scared. I really like you and I don't want to say or do anything that will make you think I'm stupid. It's better that you just know me as a customer, rather than as a person.

"Do you like Robertson Davies books? I do, I think, but I haven't read any. I saw something about him on TV a couple of weeks ago when it was the anniversary of his birth and he seems like the kind of author you and I would both like. I think that's how we're the same, what we have in common. Do you know what I mean? I mean really? I'd like to sit outside your ice cream parlour with you and talk about Robertson Davies books. We'd talk all night.

"But, you see, Tatiana, eventually I'd get hungry and I'd have to leave you. Ice cream cones and other snacks are fine for eating in front of people but I take my meals alone. Nobody should have to see that."

It was all he could muster. He lay down on the floor. He rolled around. He moaned in pain. Bloated. His breath quick and he started to sweat.

Half an hour later he felt well enough to sit up. He crawled to the living room window and struggled to his knees, rested his arms on the sill, chin on his arms. He looked at the branches of the big tree growing behind his apartment building. He looked at the row of duplexes beyond the tree. The lights of an airplane high in the sky, dwarfed by the three-quarter moon. Tatiana out there, somewhere. Somewhere in the same city as him. It would have to be enough.

COUNTING TO PRETTIDASE-NINE
or: "Getting Even with Dad"

I walk with my head down, looking for cracks in the pavement. The sidewalk is grey and rough, but my dirty white running shoes are worn and comfortable. Since I've already stepped on four cracks in the pavement with my left foot, I am trying to find four new cracks for my right foot. I have to find four cracks before I get to the hospital.

A pair of Doc Marten-clad feet suddenly blocks my progress. I stop walking. I slowly raise my head and see black jeans with worn knees, a loose leather belt, and a blue sweatshirt with the words "Daytona Beach" scrawled in yellow across its face. "Sorry," a bald man with dark glasses says as he steps out of my way. I wonder why he is shading his eyes. The sun has been hidden by thick clouds with black undersides all day, making everything around me look a little grey.

With the path clear, I begin to walk again. To avoid more near collisions, I resolve to raise my head to check for obstructions once every five steps. I can still feel the four cracks that my left foot has stepped on, physical memories lingering inside my shoe. One step, two steps, three steps. It is important to find new cracks in the pavement. Four steps, five steps, look up. My right foot feels empty and wants things evened up.

The block ends here; the sidewalk has become a short cliff overlooking the pavement of the road six inches below it. I look up and wait for the traffic to subside before attempting to cross the intersection. I look all the way down the thoroughfare and my eyes tell my brain that the street is wide where I'm standing, but gradually narrows into nothingness further down the road. There's a convenience store sign with a wide-eyed red owl on the next block that looks twice the size of an apartment building ten blocks down that I know is at least five stories tall. My father told me a long time ago that it's the shape of our eyes that makes us see things like narrowing roads and tall buildings that seem tiny from far away. He also informed me that special eyeglasses exist to correct this deficiency but he just couldn't afford to buy any for our family. When I asked him when he might be able to get some of these glasses for us, he told me we'd have them in prettidase-nine weeks. "How long is that?" I asked. "It's a long time," he said. Prettidase-nine is the numerical equivalent to the letter Z; it's the last number.

For the moment, there aren't any cars on the street except for a dark green mini-van that looks to be about the size of a dog, so I cross. The pavement on the road is darker than on the sidewalk, more black than grey. There's a thin, lightning bolt-shaped crack next to a rusting manhole cover and I adjust my gait to get my right foot to step on it. One down, three to go. I step up onto the new sidewalk, quickly check ahead for obstacles, and hop over the shadow of the red owl sign, continuing on my way. The apartment building is slowly growing taller and I can see a green bench in front of it now. Accidentally, I step on a crack I hadn't noticed with my left foot. Now it's five to one, in favour of the left. I know, right foot, I know. But don't worry, I'm sure there are more than enough cracks between me and the hospital to make everything even.

My arms swing as I walk. My father told me this is natural because humans evolved from horses and we still hold on to the distant memory of walking on four legs. Arms actually think they are doing part of the walking, he said, and we should let them swing all they want. As I pass a lamppost, the side of my swinging left hand brushes against the metal pole. The impact lingers. I stop, turn around, and pass the grey pole on my right side, trying to recreate the incident for my other hand. I miss the spot, though, and only touch the lamppost with the back of my hand, not the side, so I just stop right in front of the pole. First, I softly touch the cold pole with the back of my left hand, getting that bit of unevenness out of the way, then reach out with the side of my right hand to take care of the original problem. My hands are back to normal again, they can get back to walking. There's a crack in the pavement edging out from the base of the lamppost. Little blades of green grass are growing inside the crack. I step on it twice with my right foot, cheating a bit, I know, and now it's five to three, in favour of the left.

Sometimes it's hard to keep track of all the scores. That's why when I walk I like to take care of little problems like the one I had with the lamppost right away, so that I don't get the big ones mixed up. I used to let everything get out of whack, but that was before my father told me how the body likes everything to be equal.

I came upon him in our living room one evening when he was standing facing the wall next to the mantelpiece. He looked like he was playing a piano, the way he was tapping his fingers all over the wall. I asked him what he was doing, and he said that he was adjusting the house's central computer, but I couldn't see any buttons or anything. My mother was lying on the couch nearby, holding an empty glass on her stomach. She said, "Tell him what you're really doing," and he did.

"Tommy," my father said, "there are bees under my bed. If I don't want the bees to come out at night and sting me while I'm asleep, I have to make sure that everything is even on my body."

"Even?" I asked. I heard my mother groan and she got up from the couch, heading for the kitchen.

"Yes, even," my father continued. "You know, Tom, how sometimes you might be walking down the hall and one of your hands touches the wall? But you didn't mean for it to touch the wall? Well, if you don't want the bees to sting you at night, you have to touch the wall with your other hand, to make it even. I want to go to bed now, but I didn't keep up with everything that I did with my fingers today, so now I'm making everything even." He turned around and continued tapping the wall.

"There aren't any bees under my bed, Daddy."

"That's because you're only six years old, Tommy. The bees only start coming around when people turn seven."

My mother was back in the room, I could hear the ice clinking against the sides of her glass. "Oh, for Christ's sake, Arnold. What are you telling him now?" My father did not answer her, he just kept making everything even. My mother took a sip from her glass, wiped her chin, and lay back down on the couch.

"Do you have bees, Mommy?"

My mother closed her eyes and groaned through another sip, slightly lifting her head from the couch pillow.

She crunched some ice in her mouth. She wasn't opening her eyes so I walked over and shook her arm. Her lips were gooey wet and she smelled like the medicine she rubbed on my chest when I had the sniffles. I asked again.

"Bees? Me? No, Tommy, I killed my bees a long time ago. Your father just can't get rid of his, that's all." She then seemed to fall asleep, holding her glass on her belly.

I'm looking for cracks in the sidewalk for my right foot to step on so I can keep the bees away tonight. I've been keeping the bees away for fifteen years now. The feet are the most important to keep even, because the bees love to sting people's feet. It's five to three, in favour of the left. Somebody's tin garbage can suddenly gets in my way, and I remind myself to keep checking ahead. There's the five-storey apartment building with the green bench in front of it, only a few steps away. I stop and turn around to see how big the red owl looks now. My eyes tell my brain that the sign is about the size of a donut hole, but I know that it's actually around five feet tall. In turning, I accidentally swept the side of my right foot against the pavement while my left only touched it with the sole. I drag my left foot on its side along the sidewalk; one to one, even.

I trudge on towards the hospital. One step, two steps, three steps. They probably have those glasses to fix eyesight there, probably kept in a safe or something. Four steps, five steps, look up. There's a telephone booth at the end of the block on my side of the street, so I run across to the other. I don't want any hot lava shooting out of the receiver and burning my skin. There's another green bench on this side of the street. I find a crack in the sidewalk next to the bench and step on it with my right foot. Five to four, in favour of the left.

Running from the lava tired me out, so I decide to sit down for a bit. I turn and face the street. The centre of the bench is right behind me. I raise both arms in the air and sit down slowly on the bench. Even though I am being careful, the right side of my bum touches the bench first. I collapse into a regular sitting position, though, keeping my arms in the air, keeping them from touching anything, until I can feel the bench with my entire bum. I stand up again, my arms are tired, and sit back down, this time purposefully touching the bench with the left side of my bum first. I check my watch, it's twenty-two minutes after twelve. I check my other watch, it's the same time. They are still synchronized. Settled, I fold my hands in my lap.

Now that I am resting, I decide to use the time to get a little bit closer to prettidase-nine. It's taking a long time, but I'm determined to count all the way up to it. When I began counting to prettidase-nine, starting right from number one, Brian was still the Prime Minister. It's a lot of fun, too, because the closer I get to the end of the numbers, the funnier and funnier the names of the numbers get.

This morning, back at home, I decided to do nothing at all but go out to the backyard and count. I was determined to make some progress. Sitting on my old swing set, I got past santaclaus-nine, cornflake-nine, and gingerale-nine. After gingerale-nine came nipple. I laughed so hard when the nipple numbers came up that I only made it to nipple-six before I had to run in the house to tell my father about it.

I pushed the back door open with both of my palms at the same time, a perfect job, and went into the kitchen. I was really anxious to find my father; I wanted to show off a little bit. He's been trying to count to prettidase-nine, too, but he's way behind me, stuck at manitoba-seven. I looked around the kitchen, but my father was nowhere to be found. I noticed the cutting board was left out on the kitchen counter next to a bowl full of tomatoes. There was one tomato on the board, half of it cut into thin slices. There were drops of tomato juice on the floor, a trail, so I followed them. The little drops of tomato led to the living room, and there was more juice on the beige area rug in the middle of the floor. There wasn't anybody in the living room except for my mother, but she's always there now, in the green vase on top of the mantelpiece. I said, "Hi, I'm looking for Dad," and ran to the staircase that leads up to my parents' bedroom.

There were drops of tomato all over the stairs. I got about halfway up before I realized that I was stepping harder with my left foot than with my right, so I turned around and hopped back down, jumping on each step with both feet at the same time. I climbed to the middle of the staircase again, putting more pressure on my right foot this time, and hopped back down again to start fresh. Then I accidentally touched the wall with my left hand and had to do the same with my right. While I was fixing that up, I bit my tongue with the left side of my teeth. I took a deep breath and told myself to slow down. If I wasn't careful, I could have been stuck at the bottom of the stairs all day.

Before fixing the inequalities in my mouth, I called up to my father. "Are you up there, Dad?"

"Yes," I heard him answer. "Can you give me a hand? I'm trying to get even."

I closed my eyes and concentrated on getting everything fixed as quickly as possible. I bit down on my tongue with the right side of my teeth and was about to attempt climbing the stairs again when I realized that my eyes had been open when I made the first bite. I bit my tongue with the left side of my teeth with my eyes closed, then with the right side with my eyes open. "Tom?" my father called.

"I'm coming, Dad. I'm just having trouble getting up there again."

"All right. Take your time."

I decided to stop taking chances and hopped all the way up the stairs with both feet. I fell at the top of the stairs and had to touch my elbows to the floor a few times as I lay on my stomach. When my elbows were finally even, I got up very carefully, pressing down on the carpet with equal force in both palms, sliding both knees beneath me simultaneously, and rising slowly to a standing position. I tapped the toe of my right shoe twice on the floor, then my left once and my right again to be sure, and walked to the bedroom. I pushed the door open with both of my palms at the same time.

My father was sitting on the floor, between the end of the bed and the dresser, naked except for his underwear, sitting in a pool of red tomato juice. He was making a long cut in his right leg from his foot to his knee with the tomato knife. I saw a corresponding slash on his left leg and realized that I hadn't been following a trail of tomato juice after all.

"Are you okay, Dad?"

He looked up at me and shrugged his shoulders. His clothes, stained red, lay in a pile beside him on the floor. He held his left index finger out to me, cut to ribbons. He put the knife down on the floor and stretched out his other hand, its index finger sliced in similar fashion. "Do you think they're even?" he asked.

There were more cuts on his arms, his bare shoulders, chest, plus the new gashes in his legs. My father loves toasted tomato sandwiches but sometimes forgets to put on his cutting gloves when he gets a craving. "They look fine, Dad," I lied. "Your fingers are even." Actually, his left index finger was in slightly worse shape than his right, but I judged that a few bee stings in the night would be worth it if I could get him to stop cutting himself. I picked up the knife and passed it back and forth between my hands as I stood over him.

"Hey," my father said, "I'm not finished. Look at this cut here." He pointed to his left leg. "It's not as straight as the other one."

"I think it looks just fine, Dad." There was a lot more blood than the last time. "I think I better get a doctor for you. I think maybe I should call one from next door this time."

"No, Tom. The lava!"

"Okay. I'll go get a doctor. Just wait here."

After nipple-nine comes candlestick. After candlestick-nine comes rockgarden. After rockgarden-nine comes corncob, and after corncob-nine comes paintbrush. After that, paintbrush-one, paintbrush-two, paintbrush-three. I can't wait to find out what comes after paintbrush-nine, but I should get myself over to the hospital. I look at my watches. I've been sitting for eleven minutes, forty seconds. I'll have to wait until it's been twelve minutes to leave, the next even number after eleven. I have more time to count. Where did I leave the knife? Paintbrush-four, paintbrush-five. My watches say it's been twelve minutes now, so I get up, slowly, carefully.

I walk along the sidewalk again, the hospital is in sight now, slightly larger than a breadbox. I check for cracks in the pavement. Paintbrush-six, paintbrush-seven. There's one! I step on the crack with my right foot. The score is five to five, a tie again. Both feet feel empty. Paintbrush-eight, paintbrush-nine. The sun comes out from behind the clouds and everything around me looks a little yellow. I squint, but my left eye closes just before my right.

Maybe I'll fix that later.

Let's see, paintbrush-nine: what comes after? I wasn't expecting this. The next number is prettidase. Prettidase-one, prettidase-two.

It's nearly over.

RED PANTS ON MONKLAND

Johnny had been living in the Monkland Village for nearly eight years. Long enough, he thought, to consider himself a native. Not like the pretenders and latecomers to the neighbourhood, people who moved to Monkland Avenue only after the street's much-publicized rebirth.

When Johnny first moved to the area, there was no Second Cup to sip mochacinno and café lattés in, no Pizzédélic to munch on funky slices and sip trendy beer in, and no Benedicts to be seen in enjoying leisurely breakfasts on hungover Sunday mornings. When Johnny first moved to the area, the Monkland Tavern really was a tavern, with only one bathroom and beer that came in brown quart bottles. Now it was a refurbished, chic establishment with earth-toned walls and multi-coloured martinis in oversized glasses and a lineup out front to prove its prominence.

Johnny called up some old friends, Rachel and Ken, to come and have a taste of Monkland's refined flavour with him, and they had one of the prized terrace tables of the Ye Olde Orchard Pub. Johnny lived right upstairs, in the second-floor apartment he'd been renting for nearly eight years. The space the pub occupied had been vacant when he first moved there; a boarded-up, closed down restaurant. He was one of the few tenants to stick it out in the building after the pub opened up for business on the ground floor, boastfully claiming the noise didn't bother him. Johnny told Rachel and Ken to meet him at eight, but he'd been on the terrace since six, ensuring and reserving their place.

Johnny was drunk, but hiding it well (he thought). A kilt-clad waiter with curly hair, almost as curly as the hair on his exposed legs, arrived with their pints. Johnny's fourth Guinness, his friends' first round.

"This is a pretty cool place," Rachel said after the waiter left.

"Yep," Johnny replied, swollen pride in his voice. He turned his head back and forth, as if observing for the first time the simple, unstained wooden patio. "Who'd have thought you could get Guinness on Monkland? Not me, that's for sure, when I moved here eight years ago."

Rachel lifted her pint glass, heavy looking in her small hand, short fingers stretched to their limit, and put the rim to her lips. She took a sip, puckered her mouth and squinted her eyes like she had just sucked on a lemon, then covered up with a big smile. Ha! Johnny thought to himself, that's what you get for never leaving Laval. That's what you get for not living on the Montreal Island. That's what you get when you're not used to the taste of Guinness.

From his seat on the terrace, Johnny gazed over his realm. Across the street, Pizzédélic's overflowing terrace was packed with well-dressed, well-made people and waiters in black jeans and waitresses in black bras showing through their white T-shirts. The stairs outside of Ben & Jerry's were filled with seated ice cream cone lickers, people willing (and Johnny counted himself among them) to pay extra for flavours like Cherry Garcia and Cookie Dough because Dairy Queen and Baskin-Robbins were simply uncivilized and suburban. Johnny turned his head to look left, and the lineup outside the Monkland Tavern was healthy, full of skinny boys in skinny velvet shirts and retro, thick-framed eyeglasses, and the ladies wore capri pants and silk blouses and (Johnny knew) had tattoos on the smalls of their backs. Rachel and Ken were talking, just across the table from him, perhaps about Laval, about the latest attraction at the Récréathèque for all Johnny knew, but he wasn't listening. He was watching his neighbourhood.

Tame crowds of people walked up and down Monkland Avenue, sauntered in and out of bars, restaurants, cafés. Johnny (he wholeheartedly believed) could pick out the ones who didn't live in the area and were there to see for themselves all the good they'd heard or read about the Village. He could also pick out the ones who did live in the neighbourhood, and which ones had been living here for at least as long as Johnny, and which ones were latecomers, the catcher-uppers.

A professional-looking couple, still dressed for work at their lawyer office or their accounting firm, passed by the terrace, twisting their heads this way and that, looking like they needed a map. Tourists from Westmount, Johnny thought.

A stocky man with a leathery sunburned face, dressed in a black sweatshirt and dirty blue jeans, strode by with eyes fixed straight ahead, all destination and no journey. Native, Johnny thought. A very uncool-looking native, but a Monkland native nonetheless.

Two women strolled past the terrace. One of them was tall, wore a buttoned baby blue blazer and grey pants. The other, with curly hair, wore a simple white blouse with a beige sweater thrown over her shoulders, and black pants. They were laughing, and speaking to each other in French. Johnny's mind was blank. He didn't understand French and didn't know how to classify the women.

A couple of college-aged kids made their way loudly along the street. One had a case of twelve Sleemans hooked in his right hand. Catcher-uppers, no doubt. Latecomers living in an apartment with no balcony, Johnny told himself, and they'll drink their beer out on their fire escape tonight and throw their cigarette butts down on my street.

From across the table Ken asked him something about work, how was Johnny's job going and all that conversation-starting stuff, but Johnny stared intently at the street. He gripped both arms of his chair, pressing his nails against plastic. His hawkish eyes diligently followed the progress of one particular pedestrian. What the hell was this?

Red pants? Red pants on Monkland?! The geek was wearing red pants on Monkland and he was eating a Mr. Big chocolate bar. He was about Johnny's age, maybe a bit younger, but he didn't look like he had a job. He had little dark freckles on his cheeks and small blue eyes. His hair was long, tied in a ponytail. He wore the stupidest T-shirt Johnny had ever seen, big black letters that said LARD across the chest above a close-up, enlarged photo of what looked like a worm with a wide, gaping black mouth. Johnny wished the geek had been fat, so that he could laugh at the irony of a fat geek wearing a shirt that said LARD on it, but the geek was skinny, skinny as the skinny boys in line at the Tavern. And what was he carrying? In one hand, dangling at the geek's side, was a thin rectangular box. A board game? The geek was right in front of the terrace. Risk. Johnny compiled it all in his head: This geek is wearing red pants on Monkland, a T-shirt that says LARD on it, eats Mr. Bigs, and is going to play Risk somewhere.

"You see," Johnny said to his friends, and pointing (no longer hiding his inebriation very well), "that's the kind of shit I have to put up with around here."

"What?" Rachel asked.

"That. That shit." Johnny pointed at the geek's back, walking away, walking to his Risk game.

"What?" Rachel asked again. "That guy?"

"Yes, that guy. That geek. I bet he just moved here. Red pants! Look at him! Who the hell wears red pants anymore?"

"They're not so bad." Rachel pushed her pint glass a few inches forward, sliding it away from her on the table. "They're kind of cute. Don't you think, Ken?"

"I dunno," Ken answered, eyeing Johnny.

"Oh, come on!" Johnny said. "You would not believe the people that have been moving here lately. I've been here for eight years! This wasn't a cool place before. But now it is, and now I have to put up with shit like, like Red Pants playing Risk in the neighbourhood."

"What's Risk?" Rachel asked.

"It's a stupid war game that geeks play. Geeks who come to Monkland to be cool. I can't believe it!" The waiter came back to check on the table. Johnny finished his pint quickly. "Another," he demanded, slamming his empty glass on the table with one hand and wiping his mouth with the other. "And did you see that guy just pass? That geek with red pants?" The waiter raised one eyebrow. "He just went by!" Johnny continued. "Go look! Go in the street, you could still see him."

"It's getting late," Ken said. "We gotta go."

When Johnny woke up at eleven the next morning in his apartment of eight years on the corner of Monkland and Old Orchard, he called in sick.

The only liquid in his fridge was carrot juice from the health food store, three or four months old. He made do, dousing his pasty mouth with the thick drink.

Dressed in an undershirt and sweatpants, he leaned on his kitchen windowsill, swallowing carrot juice straight from the carton. From the window he had the same view of Monkland Avenue as from the Pub terrace below, but from a higher vantage point. He wished he had a balcony. Wished he'd had the foresight to rent a place with a balcony eight years before. He watched sleepy looking waiters and waitresses setting up tables and chairs outside Pizzédélic for the lunchtime crowd. He watched a Federal Express truck pull up and double-park right below him. Then he saw Red Pants again. "Goddammit!" Johnny blurted out loud, remembering.

Red Pants was on the other side of the street, headed the opposite way from the night before. He passed Pizzédélic. Same red pants but a different T-shirt. Johnny was disappointed and wished he could have mocked the geek for wearing the same T-shirt two days in a row. This shirt also had a message written across the chest, in big red letters: KILL EVERYONE NOW. Beneath this was a picture of a man looking at the sky, both arms raised in the air. The man in the T-shirt wore a military-style jacket and a policeman's cap. Around his neck a black and white priest's collar. The mismatched outfit, juxtaposed with the KILL EVERYONE NOW message confused Johnny and made him feel angry. He took a frustrated swig of carrot juice. Remembering more, he looked at Red Pants again. Yes, he was carrying the Risk board.

"Shit!"

Johnny dumped the rest of the carrot juice in the kitchen sink and violently pitched the empty carton in his garbage can. What's the matter with that geek? he asked himself. What's he doing walking around on Monkland with red pants and a Risk board at eleven in the morning? Doesn't he have a job? Shit, I need a beer.

He bounded down the inside stairs of his apartment building and punched the front door open, sunlight stinging his eyes. He walked to Monoprix, a depanneur just east of the Pub. In the air-conditioned environment he said an enthusiastic Hi to the guy behind the counter with the crazy frizzy hair, the guy whose name Johnny still didn't know even though he'd been buying his beer, potato chips, and *People* magazines from him for nearly eight years. He entered the small beer fridge at the back of the store. Cold in his undershirt, but he took the time to select carefully. Scoffing at Sleemans, he grabbed a six-pack of Molson Export, an old standard. As he paid, he almost asked Crazy Hair what his name was, but he stopped himself, figuring the cashier probably believed Johnny already knew his name like other Monkland natives did.

Johnny put his change in his pocket and started for the door. It opened before he got there, chiming, and Red Pants walked in with his Risk board under one arm, like a newspaper. A bag from Mulit-Mags across the street dangled from hooked fingers.

Johnny veered from his path and pretended to study the Loto-Québec display near the door, keeping a stealthy eye trained on Red Pants. The geek stopped in front of the Two-For-One chocolate bar display, scratched his chin. He reached out and came away with two Mr. Big bars. Johnny was impressed in a jealous sort of way with Red Pants's ability to grasp two chocolate bars with one hand. He read the message on Red Pants' T-shirt again and imagined himself saying something witty like, "'Kill Everyone Now?' Okay, how about if I start with you?" Red Pants turned from the chocolate bar display and approached the cash register. Johnny slithered to the door, pushed it open with his back.

He waited outside, knowing he looked like a native. His undershirt and sweatpants said it all; they spoke of familiarity and comfort with one's surroundings, they said Johnny didn't have to go far to be home again. Not like Red Pants. Red Pants had to wear T-shirts with stupid messages to make an impression. Johnny knew Red Pants was a geek underneath his funny T-shirts. The Risk board proved that much.

Red Pants left the Monoprix already digging in on one of his Mr. Bigs. Just try it, Johnny said silently to Red Pants, just try and throw that wrapper on the ground, on my street. Red Pants passed Johnny, they were inches apart for a brief moment, and headed west on Monkland. Johnny followed.

After only a few steps Red Pants stopped in front of the Tavern and chatted with one of the waitresses out on the terrace. Johnny just hung back a bit and waited. He told himself he looked like he belonged, even if simply standing and doing nothing on the sidewalk with a six-pack of Molsons in your hand wasn't exactly standard Monkland behaviour. He still had his undershirt on. He didn't have far to go.

Red Pants two-cheek kissed the waitress and continued west. Johnny started up again, too. Red Pants stopped to read the little signs and notices posted on the bus shelter in front of the Provigo. Johnny had to stop again. Red Pants finished his first Mr. Big while reading, then went around to the other side of the shelter to a garbage can. Damn, Johnny thought.

Red Pants crossed Marcil Street and unwrapped his second chocolate bar. Johnny had to wait for a couple of cars to pass before crossing the street himself, but he had Red Pants in his sights. How could he lose him, with those red pants on? Johnny quickened his pace on the other side of Marcil, but had to stop when Red Pants met somebody else on the sidewalk. Johnny recognized Red Pants's friend as one of the clerks at Avenue Video, the one with the big mouth whose endless babbling about what was "cool" and what was "lame" drove him nuts while he perused the latest releases. It figures, he thought, Red Pants runs with the Avenue Video clique. He probably gets his movies for free because he knows people who work there. Red Pants performed a complicated handshake with the video guy and continued on his way. Johnny said Hi to the clerk as he passed; he was, after all, a native and familiar with the clerks of the neighbourhood.

Again, Red Pants stopped. This time in front of Provisions Snowdon, to talk with the depanneur's Asian owner (Johnny couldn't discern and hadn't gotten around to asking, in the eight years he'd been living in the neighbourhood, what the man's exact nationality was), who was outside watering the flowers he had to sell. Johnny hung back, confident he looked natural, wondering just how Red Pants had managed to familiarize himself with so many of the locals in what couldn't have been a very long time since moving to the neighbourhood.

Red Pants handed the Risk board to the Provisions Snowdon owner who looked at the top of the box, then turned it over and inspected the bottom flap. Red Pants talked and moved his hands in the air. He threw invisible dice and made a loud explosion sound, lips vibrating. The storeowner nodded his head in understanding. Johnny opened his six-pack box and pulled out a beer. He put the box down and placed one foot on top of it, cracked the bottle open. He took a long pull and burped immediately, carrot juice gas relieved.

The Provisions Snowdon owner went back inside his store. But Red Pants just stood there. The owner came back out again, carrying a small table. A young girl, maybe ten years old, wearing an aqua T-shirt, followed him with a plastic chair in each of her hands. Johnny had seen her before, figured she was the man's daughter. The owner rearranged the flowerpots in front of his store. He placed the table in the newly freed space. The girl put the chairs down at opposite ends of the table. Red Pants put the Risk board on the table and sat down. Give me a break, Johnny thought.

The game attracted a crowd. Tourists, latecomers, and natives stopped to watch the Risk game transpire on Monkland Avenue. On his third beer, Johnny stood at the front of the growing crowd, disbelieving. "This could take hours," he heard a native man say to his native girlfriend, "two-man Risk could go on for days!" The crowd laughed and gasped at this announcement. Johnny stewed.

Red Pants's armies were concentrated in Australia. He had a scattering of soldiers in most of the Asian countries, and a horde placed strategically on Kamchatka, poised to cross the Bering Strait and attack Alaska at any time, the harbinger of an invasion and eventual sacking of North America. The Provisions Snowdon owner was a Risk novice. His men were all over the board, and his largest contingent sat uselessly in the middle of Africa, on Congo and Madagascar. With his next move, the owner began a futile attack on the Middle East from Egypt. He had only four men to Red Pants's twenty. The young girl came out with two cans of Coke and a bag of Cheesies for the players. Some people in the crowd asked if she could bring them Coke and Cheesies as well. The girl went back inside the store to fill the orders. Johnny couldn't believe it. Red Pants would be famous. Nobody cared that he wasn't from here. Nobody cared that Johnny had been living in the neighbourhood for eight years and felt comfortable enough in his surroundings to drink beer in an undershirt on the street. He'd had enough.

"Don't do it," Johnny said. The Provisions Snowdon owner looked up at him, mouth open a crack. "Don't attack there, you'll lose for sure and open up Africa for attack. You'll lose everything."

"All right, man," Red Pants rapped enthusiastically. Johnny looked at him, looked closely at his face for the first time. He had chocolate stains in the corners of his mouth. "Cool," Red Pants went on. "You know Risk?" His reached out to the board, cleared it of all the armies with a sweep of his hand. "Could use a third person. Wanna play?"

Johnny felt the crowd watching his next move. The Provisions Snowdon owner popped a Cheesie in his mouth and licked his finger. Red Pants stared at Johnny, waiting for his reply. Johnny looked at the chocolate stains again. He reached inside his beer box and grabbed the neck of one bottle. He pulled it out and clasped it firmly with his fingers, pointing the bottom end of the bottle at Red Pants's face. "Have a beer?" he heard himself ask.

The Provisions Snowdon owner called out something in his native tongue to the open door of his store. The man's daughter appeared almost immediately with another chair and some brown paper bags. Johnny scratched his armpit. "What colour?" Red Pants asked. Johnny stared at him dumbly. "What colour do you want to be, dude?"

"Red. Can I be red?"

NOT YOUR PERSONAL ASHTRAY

With the edge of the glass between his pursed lips, allowing a slow stream of water to flow into his mouth, wetting his tongue and cooling his throat, Roger watches Geneva reach beneath her desk to buzz the courier in. The office door clicks and the navy blue-clad messenger enters and places a red, white and blue envelope on the front desk, then hands Geneva his clipboard. His company baseball cap looks well worn, worked on at night, at home, Roger speculates, fitting the man's head as if he had left the womb with it on. He flirts with Geneva, leaning his arms on the desk now, and Roger, the glass still to his lips, not drinking anymore, only smelling his own breath, watches the back of her blond hair bob with polite laughter. She hands the pad back and the courier stands up straight again, but he's still talking. He's got his signature, Roger thinks, what else does he want? Geneva laughs so loudly now, so genuinely, that everybody else in the office looks up, notices. Roger pretends not to watch anymore and puts his glass down, empty, half on the plastic desk pad and half on the colour photograph of his mother he's been meaning to frame for the last six months. He pushes it off of the picture's surface before any unseemly rings can form.

Roger looks up again, the courier has finished his subtle harassment and is turning to leave, he has more packages under his arm. Roger sits up a bit in his seat, walks him out the door with his eyes, notices how hairy the backs of the young man's calves are and what an immaculate ironing job has been done on his shorts. Geneva swivels in her chair and stands with the newly arrived envelope in her hand. She is wearing a beige plaid skirt and no stockings, brown low-heels looking comfortable somehow. A long, thin silver chain bounces on her yellow blouse as she walks directly toward Roger. She waves the envelope playfully in the air, with a mother's teasing "I'm gonna get you" look on her face. A plastic braid keeps the hair out of her eyes — green-coloured contact lenses today — but one small collection of strands has escaped and hangs down the right side of her face. Her cheeks are white beneath the subtle touch of blush applied to them, her lips are small, and, with her mouth slightly open, her two front teeth rest gently on her bottom lip.

Roger gets up quickly, a metal clang resounding from the impact his waist and thighs make with his desk. He puts one hand on his chair, then both on the desk, as if checking for injuries, instinctively plunges his forefinger into the bridge of his nose, to push up the eyeglasses that he's not even wearing, and returns his hands to the desk.

"Don't get up," he stutters. "I was just going to fill my water glass." His hands search, find the glass.

"Aren't you sweet?"

"Really, it's no trouble." He meets her halfway.

"Here you go, big shot," she hands him the envelope. "Only the big shots get FedEx, you know."

Roger swallows and regurgitates a giggle from somewhere inside of him, clears his throat, and pats his left breast. Geneva is already at his desk, and returns with his glasses. He accepts them, gratefully, clumsily, slips them over his ears, now ready to read.

"Those really make you look cute, you know."

Of course she says that, Roger thinks. She helped him pick out the glasses at the quick-serve optometry centre near the Métro station last winter. They had met by chance, leaving the office for lunch separately and then finding each other in the same line at the food court. He looked around for signs of a boyfriend, a date, a friend of hers, whoever was eating with her. No such person emerged. Over MSG-free Japanese combos served on Styrofoam plates he disclosed to her his quandary over choosing new frames for his reading glasses. It felt strange, letting her in on such intimate knowledge, but it just came out. Even stranger when she practically took him by the arm and, after holding the garbage can flap open for him to brush his plate and plastic utensils off his tray, marched him to the optometry centre.

Inside, he let her take over. It felt natural, familiar to do so, as she picked out various shapes and sizes of frames for him to try on. There was laughter when he put on a thick, horn-rimmed pair, she saying that her father used to wear ones just like that, and he thinking, but unable to say, the same. She practically fell over, laughing herself silly when, on a whim, she modelled a classic grandma pair of silver-rimmed glasses on herself. She came at him, giggling, slapped him on the shoulder, hyperventilating. Then her silver necklace became entangled with a button on his shirt collar. There was an uncomfortable but enjoyable minute of dislodging, she holding her breath to keep from laughing, coughing up soya-smelling chuckles throughout, he hot in the ear lobes and nervous. "Don't tell anybody about this, Roger," she joked, half seductively, when they finally freed each other.

Geneva settled on a small pair of glasses for him, smaller than Roger would have ever dared wear, with oval rims. She told him he'd fit in as easily on the terrace of a St. Denis café as in the office with these glasses. He trusted her judgment, had none of his own, and put his money down.

"What are you doing for lunch today?" she asks, reading the address label of the Federal Express envelope over his shoulder.

"Lunch?" He looks at his watch. "Lunch . . . I, I brought a lunch today."

"You always bring a lunch, Roger. When are we going to go to lunch again?"

"I have to fill my water glass," he spits out, not even looking back at her.

He feels her watching him walk out the door with the envelope under his arm and his damned water glass in his hand.

Roger strides quickly down the hall, blue walls, grey carpet, less familiar than the office, more anonymous. He passes doors to the offices of other companies in the building, the elevators, and turns the corner. He opens the washroom door just wide enough to slip inside, and closes it by leaning back against the door, one palm flat against its wooden surface, the other still holding the glass. The envelope pops out from under his arm from the leaning and falls on the checkered tile floor. He doesn't pick it up right away, he's too busy breathing.

He is accosted by his own image in the long mirror in front of him, running the length of the sink and counter, the counter that Roger knows is stained with little globs of wasted liquid soap. It's always like that. He looks at his face in the mirror and thinks his head is shaped like an acorn. His hair is thinning in the front, showing off his entire forehead and a good portion of his exterior scalp. Where his brown hair begins it stands, not straight up but at an acute angle with the top of his skull, without any aid from teasing or hair care products. With the glasses his eyes are not as boring as he usually finds them, brown, nothing. His bony cheeks are populated by tiny specks of the black stubble that always returns to his face well before lunch. He puts one finger to his large, flat lips, bites at the nail.

He bends to pick up his envelope, taking care to make as little contact between the bathroom floor and his fingers as possible. He straightens, is confronted with himself again in the mirror. He looks at his V-neck sweater, dark and light checkers of green, the beige collar of his shirt underneath, and the knot of his brown woollen tie. His pants are brown, flannel, and he can feel the thin brown socks around his damp, sweaty feet, encased in the brown pair of topsiders that are just the right size so that he never has to tie or untie them when putting them on or taking them off. He approaches the mirror, looks deeply into his own eyes, their size magnified by the glasses, then finds a clean place on the counter for his water glass and envelope. He rushes past the urinal and escapes into the toilet stall.

Roger is disgusted, appalled. The water in the toilet is yellow, unflushed, and the remains of a smoked cigarette float on the surface. The butt is in two pieces: the foam portion of the filtre, dislodged from its soaked paper sheath, and the tobacco-laden cylinder with its black, burnt out triangular end. A thin stream of brown tar snakes out from the tip, motionless in the water. The black plastic toilet seat is inundated with grey and black cigarette ashes that lie among three tiny liquid puddles of unknown origin. There are more ashes on the floor, and more puddles, and the whole place suddenly smells like the all-night donut shop when there are no empty seats in the non-smoking section for Roger. "Dammit," he says, out loud. He hates the fact that he must share this bathroom with the other men from his office, and the men from all of the offices on the eleventh floor. They know they're not supposed to smoke in here.

He thinks of the men that lounge around outside the building in spring and summer, their shirtsleeves rolled up to beat the heat, ties flapping in the breeze, flicking ashes and butts all over the pavement. He tries to remember their faces, guessing at who the guilty party might be. He thinks of them crowding the entrance in the fall and winter, staying warm with him forced to breathe their stench, the whole lobby smelling like the inside of an old, empty beer bottle. Why should smokers take more breaks than the rest of us, he asks himself for the umpteenth time. I take breaks to relieve myself and to fill my water glass, I take care of the basics. They take breaks to meet their chemically enhanced needs and feel perfectly justified in doing so. He stares at the toilet seat again, cannot believe that somebody on the eleventh floor has the gall to leave it in such a state. He exits, punching the stall door open, fills his water glass, retrieves his envelope, and marches back to the office.

Geneva buzzes him in, he avoids her eyes, though he knows she's looking at him. Roger sits back down at his desk and takes a small sip of water. He completely avoids the photograph this time, placing his glass on the corner of his desk with the small jade plant. He can't work, Geneva is after him about lunch again and the bathroom is filthy. He removes his glasses, rubs his eyes, and turns to look out his window. He rests his chin in one palm and sighs. It is bright outside; the tinted glass of his window is bluer than usual. He looks down on the Trans-Canada Highway, the raised portion where Cote de Liesse begins beneath it. A few cars fly by in both directions, little toy cars from the eleventh floor. Lazy, late people, Roger thinks. There are trucks and vans, too. They're okay, they're supposed to be there. Behind the autoroute, peeking over its elevated lanes, is the big orange Salada sign, the giant Kraft logo, and the brown billboard with a smoked meat sandwich and pickle advertising Les Aliments T. Lauzon. The Hygrade kids chow down perpetually on their hot dogs. Watching over all, huge, green, is the northern slope of Mount Royal.

The trees and bushes mix together from this distance, the mountain looks vital, alive. Roger likes to look at the mountain. He stares at his two favourite landmarks: the Université de Montréal tower and St. Joseph's Oratory. He likes them equally, each beautiful in its own way. His mother liked the tower best, she once told him as they drove home from the Laurentians, the mountain suddenly visible as they sped through Laval on the autoroute. "Which one do you like?" He didn't know.

The Université tower stands noble and erect, shooting straight up into the sky. With its lean stem and rounded triangular apex, Roger thinks it looks like a beige torpedo readied for launch. From up high on the eleventh floor, it looks small enough for one of his hands to grasp it all the way around, his thumb meeting and resting on his four fingers. He is proud that Montreal has such a monument to impress visitors with, thinks he would definitely point it out if he ever had a visitor.

The Oratory, with Brother André's preserved heart stored within, is softer, rounder, not as snatching to the eye as the tower, but just as magnificent. The old green dome appears to lounge about the trees, flopping out as if by its own choice. A crucifix is centred on its coned roof, all so small from Roger's perch, small enough to reach out and cup in his palm. He thinks he would like to take somebody to the Oratory, a visitor, and show them the three sets of stairs, explain the religious significance of the centre stairs, tour the cathedral and gift shop, gaze upon the many abandoned crutches and canes kept behind glass, and, of course, pay homage at the little iron case where the amputated heart of the man who built the place is kept. He thinks Geneva might like to go. No, she would laugh at the idea. He turns away from the window, away from the tower and the Oratory, planning to get a little work done.

But his bladder is full. The painful yearning for relief returns his thoughts to the bathroom, the filthy bathroom. He has to do something about the lack of respect the eleventh-floor washroom is being treated with. He hates the smokers he knows are downstairs, or maybe in the bathroom right now. He imagines ten of them, good-looking, confident men, crammed in the toilet stall like 1950's pranksters in a phone booth, smoking, ashing, laughing, mocking him. He sees their groomed, full heads of hair, their white teeth, chiselled cheek- and jawbones. Laughing, jostling each other in the cramped quarters, blowing smoke everywhere. He hates them.

Roger places a sheet of white typing paper in front him and grabs a black felt marker from among the pens and pencils in the coffee mug at the edge of his desk. He looks up at the ceiling, taps the pen against his chin a few times, then uncaps it. He writes, furiously, a steady stream of angry ink flowing from the marker onto the paper. He puts a period to his last sentence and reads over his work. Geneva is coming over.

"What's that?"

"This? This is a notice to those people who think the men's washroom is their own personal ashtray. I'm not going to stand for it anymore, Geneva."

"You're not?" She seems surprised by Roger's sudden air of certainty. He likes that she's surprised, but doesn't know exactly why. "Can I see?" she asks.

Roger hands her his notice. She reads.

THIS IS <u>NOT</u> YOUR PERSONAL ASHTRAY.
Please do not smoke or leave your ashes here.
We share this space.

"Wow, you really mean it, Roger. Are you going to put this up in the bathroom?"

"Yes," he rises, clanging his thighs against the bottom of the desk again. "I'm not going to take it anymore."

He marches to the door, puts one hand on the handle, then hears her call out: "You want some scotch tape?"

He takes two small pieces of tape gratefully, and walks out into the blue hallway. He pictures the bathroom in his mind, mulls over the different places he can place his sign, tries to decide where it would be most visible. If I can take a stand like this, he thinks, maybe I can ask Geneva to the Oratory. He straight-arms the washroom door open and is hit full on by a long, low-lying cloud of cigarette smoke.

The paper in his hands feels suddenly large, obvious. He holds it behind his back with both hands. A man stands to the side of the mirror, his back to Roger, using the urinal. He's wearing a black woolly sweater. His khaki pants are pulled down a bit, to just beneath his backside, exposing a pair of murky green briefs. Roger is reminded of the kids in grade school who got teased and taunted for not knowing how to pull down their zipper instead of their pants in front of a urinal. Was I one of those kids? He can't remember. The underwear is very loose around the man's buttocks, particularly sagging in the middle. Roger can see small, prickly black hairs and a few red blemishes on the small portion of exposed thighs. He turns to leave.

"Hey, wait," the man says. "I'm almost done."

Roger stands at the door, sideways to the man, looking at the floor. He peeks up, sees the man's head is turned to the side now, looking at Roger, a burning cigarette with a long, teetering ash dangling from his mouth. Roger does not recognize his face, cannot place it among the extra-long-break-takers from downstairs.

The man jiggles, pulls up his pants, zips, buttons, drops his cigarette into the urinal, hissing, and turns to face Roger while he ties his belt. Roger looks down again. He sees ashes on the floor, looks the man in the eye. His mouth moves to speak, to personally inform the man of the essence of the notice he came to post, but nothing comes out.

"Do you work on this floor?" the man asks, his back to Roger again, washing his hands, dripping liquid soap all over the counter. "I don't think I've seen you before."

"Yes, at August Sales." Roger is relieved to speak, to talk about anything but what he had come to the bathroom for. He listens to the silence that follows. "Do you, um, work on this floor, too?"

"No, I work up on the fourteenth. It's a little weird, but I prefer this bathroom, so I come down here sometimes." He dries his hands with a paper towel. He extends one hand. "I'm Gene."

Roger offers his right hand, keeping the left behind his back, clasping the notice. "Roger." Gene's hand is soft, moist, but his grip is firm.

"Nice to meet you, Roger. Well," he bends a little and waves ceremoniously at the urinal, "It's all yours."

"Um, thank you." Roger takes a step toward the urinal, his bladder readying itself for deflation. He forgets the nature of the notice and holds it in front of his waist.

"What's that?" Gene asks, pointing.

Roger looks at the pointing finger, at his waist region, aghast. The he realizes that Gene means the paper. "Oh, nothing."

"Let me see." He has a new cigarette in the corner of his mouth. He lights it with a click and a snap from his silver lighter. "What have you got there?" He places himself in front of Roger, quietly, but rigidly. He puts his hand out for the paper, Roger feels hypnotized, surrenders the notice. His bladder screams at him, threatening him with contractions. He isn't listening.

"*. . . not your personal ashtray*. Oh, I didn't know this bothered you. I'm sorry." Gene flicks his wasted cigarette into the urinal, hissing again. "You were going to hang this up, weren't you?"

"Well, um, it's really not that big of a deal. I mean, yes, I don't like the ashes on the floor, on the seat, but the smell isn't all that bad, really. You know, I don't really need to put that up, you can just throw it out. Please."

"Hey, Rog, don't get all tied up in knots like that. It's okay, I understand." Gene approaches Roger, puts one of his soft, firm hands on his shoulder. His light brown bangs and blue eyes are right in his face. Roger smells his breath, rancid, like a tar truck. He feels Roger's hand squeeze his shoulder, gently, becoming a massage. He twists, but Gene doesn't release his grip.

"Excuse me," Roger says, "I really have to use the toilet."

"Okay, okay," Gene lifts his hand from Roger's shoulder, keeps it in the air, innocuous.

Roger shuffles to the urinal, presses his body as close as possible to the porcelain, unzips his pants and cups both of his hands to shroud himself. He waits to feel the relief he yearns for, but his bladder is wreaking revenge on him now, and Gene is still standing there. How can he go when that, that harassing man is right behind him?

"Just whistle a bit, think about a waterfall, it'll come then."

"I can take care of myself, thank you," Roger barks at the ceramic wall.

But he does think about water: the fountain at Square Victoria, the bust of the old Queen. His mother liked to visit Queen Victoria on Sundays. He always had to go with her, drinking tea from a thermos with her, always with her, waiting until she was tired enough to decide to go home. The ritual began when he was a child, and before Roger realized that he had grown to be a man he was still doing it. Still taking trips to the Laurentians with Mother ("Let's go see the leaves"), watching *Perry Mason* and, in later years,

Matlock, with her at night ("Oh, I wonder who did it?"), going for endless walks ("My knees just kill, let's sit here for a while"), and always, always, drinking tea on Sundays with Queen Victoria ("My Auntie Vie met her once during a parade, you know"). Roger empties himself, wishing Gene would just go away.

He sidesteps to the sink, plunges his hands under warm water. Gene is there in the mirror, lighting another cigarette. He hooks it in the corner of his mouth, eyes squinting, and turns around, holding Roger's notice against the wall. "How about right here?"

Roger doesn't bother to dry his hands and snatches the sign away from Gene. "You're mocking me," he hisses, surprised at his own boldness.

"No, no, seriously," Gene says, "This'll be my last time. I won't do it here anymore. I swear." He takes a long drag, the cigarette buttressed between his thumb and forefinger.

Roger pulls the door open and walks quickly down the hall, the paper flapping in his hand at his side. He hears Gene, "Aw c'mon, Rog! Hey Rog! Wait!"

He glances behind him, sees Gene is following, without the cigarette. Roger increases his pace, and when he gets around the corner, out of sight, he jogs. The office door clicks at the exact moment he grabs the handle, as if Geneva has been waiting for him, only him, vigilantly. "Hey," she remarks as he flies by her desk, "You didn't put up your sign."

Roger retreats to his desk, feels protected by it. This is where he's supposed to be, this is where he belongs. His papers, pens, telephone, Post-Its, calendar, the jade plant — they're all familiar. Posting signs in public washrooms is not. He can't believe the notion to do something crazy like that ever entered his mind. Everything would have gone on normally if he'd just stayed where he belonged. Done what he was supposed to do. He would have been safe. He crumples the notice and tosses it into the wastepaper basket under the desk.

He looks out the window again, right at the domed Oratory. He thinks of his mother, her funeral just two months ago. He didn't even tell Geneva that she'd died. He didn't know if he was allowed. His mother wasn't there anymore to tell him what was okay to do and what wasn't. She didn't leave instructions. He remembers how he imagined soon after the funeral what it would be like to tell Geneva, and how he felt comforted in that fantasy. But was it okay to really do it?

He hears the office door click. Gene is coming in. He's talking to Geneva, talking to her the same way the courier talked to her before. All suave. Roger is angry, scared, and embarrassed all at the same time. Gene is still talking to Geneva, but he's looking beyond her. He's scanning the office. Roger tilts his head toward the surface of his desk, hooks his hand to his forehead like he's shading himself from the sun, and watches Gene as stealthily as he can. Their eyes meet. Gene waves. Roger can't look away now. Gene comes around Geneva's desk. She stands up, steps in front of him, shakes her head, No, you can't go over there. She glances back at Roger, quickly, but then Gene's hand is on her shoulder. She twists her head to look at it, as if an insect were crawling there. Roger sees Gene's fingers move in unison, kneading the flesh surrounding Geneva's shoulder blade. Roger shoots up, clanging his waist against the underside of his desk.

Geneva takes one step back, breaking Gene's grip on her, then in one fluid motion steps forward again and slaps Gene full on across the face. He recoils, presses his palm lightly to his reddened cheek. Roger stands beside his desk, frozen. Gene's eyes find his, looks at him like he's an old buddy betrayed, and Roger doesn't move. Can't. Deep down he knows he should move, do something, but it's too automatic to wait for somebody to tell him exactly what he should do. Two other men from the office are marching toward Gene. They escort him out the door, go with him into the hall.

Geneva just stands there, looking down, her back to Roger, her arms hugging her sides. Roger feels his left foot move first, then his right. He's walking toward her. He's deciding it's the right thing to do. When he gets close he changes his direction slightly, a diagonal line out from where she stands, then a diagonal line in, so that he arrives before her at an angle that won't startle her. She's still looking at the floor. He touches her arm ever so lightly with the tips of his fingers and bends his head to get his eyes at her level. Her lips tremble slightly, and she's tearing.

"Maybe we should take an early lunch," he says.

"Thank you." She reaches for his hand on her arm and clasps it, hard.

He holds the office door open. She passes him, goes out. Roger is right behind her.

OTHER PEOPLE'S SHOWERS
or: "No Soap, Radio"

With a cigarette hooked in the corner of his mouth, Perry waited outside the Kentucky Fried Chicken's front door. The cool, still November air and passive grey sky combined to create a pleasant contrast to the hustle and bustle of the inside; a welcome reprieve from the heat of twelve oil fryers working in unison, the dull, biting glare of yellow food lamps, and the pandemonium of beeping timers and ringing cash registers.

In his mind's eye, Perry could see a long beige station wagon with pseudo-wood panelling barrelling down Labelle Boulevard, his girlfriend Tanya at the wheel. She flew past the mall, past the Speedy Muffler, and slowed for a red light beside Mike's Submarines. Perry imagined how she looked comically out of place; a nineteen- going on twenty-year-old speeding innocently through indiscriminate lane changes in the quintessential family car from another decade while the Indigo Girls sang out through an open window.

Then Perry's mind showed him a sweaty, dandruff-infested, mustached man behind the wheel of a light blue hatchback. The man's jeans were so tight he had to leave the top button open in order to breathe comfortably. Perry imagined the man angry, angry because Tanya's station wagon had cut off his car as they both passed the Telicino video store. He sped up to keep pace with the offending driver, eyeing the approaching red traffic light as an opportunity to articulate his disfavour with a symbolic hand gesture. Trying to choose between a shake of the fist and a raised middle finger, the hot and bothered man screeched to a stop alongside the station wagon. He looked across but felt his throat buckle. His right hand, readied for a muted expression of angry emotion, fell limp into his lap, useless and numb.

Perry created a glimpse of the future for himself, when the man, at home and alone, would throw himself on the floor, initiating a contained blizzard of dandruff in his living room, and weep.

Tanya sat patiently at the light, unaware of her annoying driving habits. Perry could see her milky skin, soft and young, clinging supplely to raised cheekbones beneath brightly blinking green eyes. She reached to scratch her slightly upturned nose in a way that showed she had little concern for, or was even aware of, the possibility of onlookers confusing her itch for a pick. Tanya's hair, shoulder-length and coloured like a field of dying wheat, had been whipped about by the wind, and two thin strands were held inside the moisture of the corner of her mouth.

Perry's eye on the future saw the sweaty man wailing like an animal and pounding his living room floor with his fists, haunted by the memory of small red lips, pursing and unpursing in an unconscious attempt to free captured hairs. Perry could see how the sweaty man saw Tanya's lips. The man will never flip off another driver. He will never again take that risk. He will avoid at all costs the cold and biting nausea that went along with the slightest consideration of rendering insult upon the face of innocence, the face of beauty. Perry imagined his girlfriend's lips again, and smiled.

Perry could see all of this, past-present-future, despite the fact that he was at least a kilometre away from the cars, and at least an hour away from the mustached man's emotional breakdown. He wore a light autumn jacket over his Kentucky Fried Chicken uniform and held his paper hat in one hand. The outfit had a different feel to it out there, outside the restaurant at the end of a shift. The uniform didn't carry the same weight of pressure and responsibility that it did for Perry when he was inside, his hands caked with white flour while the oily stench of chicken and fries dripped from the walls and from his brow. The only weight Perry could feel now was the laggardly pleasant flow of nicotine rolling in his lungs and in his head. The cigarettes that came after work were decidedly different from the ones Perry smoked at other times. It was not the physical properties of the cigarettes themselves — he did not change brands to attain different tar levels, he did not switch from filtered to plain, and, despite an affection for the occasional menthol, he didn't save the minty greens for this special time. It was, however, the temporary feeling of autonomy that Perry felt in the first few minutes at the end of a working day that changed smoking. In those moments, while he could still feel that he was at the end of a shift and had not yet begun to think about the next one beginning, all of Perry's other responsibilities paled and faded because it felt so damned good just to not be at work. The air was cleaner, the sun more charitable, and the nicotine buzz was slightly more intense.

It was here outside, away from work, that Perry could think about where other people were and what they were doing in places where he could not actually see them. He imagined Tanya, on her way to pick him up. He imagined his younger brother, Greg, at home watching Saturday afternoon wrestling. He imagined a Japanese autoworker named Tom Yoritomo on the other side of the world asleep in his bed. Seeing people in his head that he didn't personally know was a lot more interesting than thinking about his friends and family. Perry could see himself standing and smoking on the solid soil of the Northeastern portion of the continent and feel others sharing the same landmass thousands of kilometres away. He saw the fields, the cities, the plains, and the mountains as his mind travelled west to visit a sales clerk tending to customers in a downtown Vancouver Gap franchise. Even more thrilling was the vastness of ocean to the east of him that led to a McDonald's maintenance employee, diligently painting the walls of a stock room in Frankfurt. "I wonder if it's true that they serve beer in German McDonald's," Perry mused.

Deep down, when watching a retired insurance broker chopping a cord of wood in the white snow-capped mountains of Wyoming, or a sweaty man with a dandruff problem crying in a living room, Perry knew that he was not actually "seeing" events as they happened. He did not have any superhuman powers (although the idea of having the ability to become invisible was very appealing and Perry thought a lot about how much fun it would be to walk unseen into a classroom and cause bloody havoc for his old teachers by making chalk and erasers seem to float just by carrying them around in his invisible hands, and about what a laugh would ensue when he would lift Mrs. Ferderko's long dress over her head, exposing her girdle for all the class to see, and about all the shitheads that ever laughed at him or left him out of parties that he would smack and punch and kick), and Perry accepted this deficiency. Even if he couldn't physically get away, he wasn't about to imprison his mind in his immediate surroundings.

Perry saw Tanya pull into the Kentucky Fried Chicken parking lot (for real) and took a last haul from his cigarette. He crushed it beneath one greasy shoe. He exhaled as he sat down in the passenger seat. Despite the damaging effects of second-hand smoke, Tanya patted Perry's knee and gave him a kiss on the mouth. Perry felt Tanya's lips, the lips of innocence, press gently against his own. He lingered in their velvety softness. He could not decide if her lips were wet or dry, so flawless was the balance between the two extremes. He wanted, needed, to open her mouth. He wanted to press his own lips, armed with the teeth behind them, against hers and, like a trained dog might whir its head to catch a snack placed on its snout, flick his head upward, working the lock of Tanya's top lip. He held himself back, though, suppressing the animal, knowing from experience that it was not for him to decide when the mouth of innocence, of beauty, should open. Their mouths parted without a sound, a silent smack, and Perry felt a small dynamite detonation in his chest when he saw a glittering strand of silky saliva caught between his bottom and her top lip. He tried in vain to follow Tanya's head as she pulled away from his, hoping to keep the flickering liquid bond between them intact. He felt the rope explode and basked in the tiny spray that washed against his chin, the sweet melange of his own and Tanya's spit. Perry began to silently review strategies for getting more out of Tanya later on.

"I picked up your clothes at your house and you can take a shower at my house before we go," Tanya said.

"Thanks," Perry replied, a little distracted.

"Your brother still acts really weird around me."

"Brian or Greg?" Perry began to pay more attention.

"Greg. When I was waiting for your Mom to get your stuff he came up to me karate chopping and talking like an idiot."

"Was he making his mouth move all fast? Like, faster than he was really talking?"

"Yeah."

"That's his new thing. He's pretending to be a kung fu fighter in a dubbed movie."

"I know but it's weird."

"I'm not saying anything to him 'cause he's still bugging me about the last time I yelled at him about this crap. When you phoned and said 'Can I speak to Perry?' and he said 'I dunno, can you?' I gave him shit and now he says that I said that he's gonna be 'the cause of this breakup!' As if I ever said that."

"That's so cute!"

"I never said that!"

"I know, but it's cute."

Perry fumbled through the cassettes in Tanya's glove compartment. "Do you still have my White Stripes in here?"

"I'm listening to my music!"

"I'm pretty hungry, can you go through the Drive-Thru somewhere?"

"We're eating in like two hours and Michelle is making burritos."

"Wait — we're going to her place? I thought they were coming to your house."

"I told you we were going there. Didn't you listen to me?"

"Are your parents taking their own car?"

"Why, do you have to be home early? It's not like we're going downtown or anything. Your parents know it's just my aunt's house."

"It's not my parents . . . what if *I* want to leave early?"

"Then get your own car."

"Mm."

After a short ride during which the Indigo Girls did most of the rest of the talking, Tanya parked the station wagon in her parents' two-car garage. Just before going in the house, Perry squeezed her left buttock and received a playful swat on the hand for his effort, a sure sign that any lingering animosities had been left in the car. Mr. McMillen was in the living room reading a magazine with the television on. A British soap opera was playing, so Perry surmised that his girlfriend's father had been watching some other program on the same channel and simply hadn't bothered to turn off the set when it was over. "I guess some people don't know that the OFF button can be a choice," he thought to himself, laughing inside. This brief moment of superiority fizzled with the sound of Mr. McMillen's voice.

"Hi there, Perry. How are things at the KFC?"

"Just fine. We cooked some chickens today." It was a crude and uncomfortable attempt at a joke, but it was the only way Perry knew how to talk with the man, with the father of the girl he wanted to have sex with in a car before the day was over. Mr. McMillen offered a polite laugh. He immediately switched to a friendly sarcastic tone that matched Perry's, which was the best way he knew how to communicate with the kid whose tongue he suspected of being inside his daughter's mouth on numerous occasions.

In this way, Perry and Tanya's father had been able to engage themselves in conversation for the past ten months or so without ever actually talking.

"Looks like your pants are a little dirty there, Perry."

Perry glanced down to see numerous streaks of white flour on the thighs of his navy blue polyester uniform pants. "Yeah, I know. It's just that this new guy kept wiping his hands on me today."

Mr. McMillen laughed again, this time even more politely. "Well, you better change before Tanya wipes her hands of you!"

Perry and Mr. McMillen forced themselves to smile and laugh until Tanya and her mother walked into the room. Tanya was carrying a large blue towel that she handed to Perry. "Here you go, babe." It was clean and smelled strongly of lemony fabric softener sheets, a foreign but pleasing scent to Perry. "We're going to the store to get wine while you take your shower."

"Um, are you all going?" Perry asked, deliberately blinking his eyes, hoping Tanya would understand the hidden, libidinous meaning behind his question.

"Yeah . . . I guess." Tanya looked confused, studying Perry's eyes.

"Well, it's just that—"

"Okay, let's go," Mr. McMillen suddenly ordered, rising from the couch with the magazine in his hand.

"All right, Dad," Tanya replied. Her expression changed abruptly, a look of comprehension washing over her face. She winked at Perry, shrugged apologetically, and blew him a kiss as she followed her parents to the door. Perry pretended to catch the kiss on his cheek and lowered his head, exaggerating his dejection. Tanya laughed and shut the door. Perry turned the television off.

There was something exciting to Perry about being left alone in somebody else's house. It wasn't as good as having his very own place, tops on Perry's list of aspirations, but at least when nobody was home he didn't have to worry if his shirt was untucked or make sure there was a coaster under his glass. He wanted to smoke but doing so in the middle of the McMillens' living room was out of the question. He told himself to wait until later, in the shower, where the smoke would blend nicely with the steam in the bathroom fan and his cigarette butt could be disposed of without detection into the shower drain. First, however, Perry did as he usually did when he found himself unchaperoned in a house: head straight for the kitchen. "Just a little sandwich before they get back," he thought.

Opening up the McMillens' refrigerator, Perry was amazed, as he always was, by the quantity of food and incredible selection inside. At home, his own parents' fridge was filled with monstrosities; blasts from the past like six-month-old taco sauce in a jar that was impossible to close properly because there was dry sauce caked all around its rim, or leftover spaghetti and meat balls in a cereal bowl that had turned orange and hard as rock because it had never been covered. In the McMillens' fridge, all leftovers and opened sandwich meat packages were carefully sealed inside Ziploc bags, while in his own fridge at home Perry felt lucky if the ham was wrapped in paper towels.

Perry began to compile the necessary ingredients for his sandwich on the counter: cheese, lettuce, alfalfa sprouts, mortadella, pickles, tomato, turkey. He paused to consider the spreading condiments. He could have taken his usual combination of mustard and mayonnaise but he found a jar of Hellman's Dijonnaise spread, pre-mixed mustard and mayonnaise. Unable to decide, Perry grabbed all three jars. He then made his way to the opposite end of the kitchen counter where all the bread was kept in a basket. "Nobody ever has fucking sourdough," he thought as he checked out the selection. He opened a package of pumpernickel, took out two slices and turned back toward the fridge. Then he thought better of it and grabbed the rest of the loaf. "Something to snack on while I'm *making* the sandwich," he thought, reaching for the butter dish on the counter.

With a mouthful of butter-on-bread "snack," Perry took out the McMillens' cutting board and grabbed a steak knife. With nobody at home, Perry chewed with his mouth open and farted at will. He cut three thin slices of tomato and hid the rest at the bottom of the garbage can. Again farting and licking a finger, Perry opened the Ziploc containing a fresh-looking round of mozzarella cheese. "Saputo, no doubt," he thought and cringed at the memory of his own fridge stocked only with generic-brand processed cheese slices. He cut himself a thick wedge of mozzarella. Taking another bite of his snack, Perry opened the jar of Dijonnaise spread and used the steak knife to distribute the product on a slice of pumpernickel. Perry spread a very thin layer of mustard on the other slice of bread and reached out for the grand prize. "Mmmm, mayonnaise," he said out loud in a deliberate Homer Simpsonesque voice.

After almost laughing at his own joke, Perry recalled staying home from school one day as a young boy, ailed by the sickness his parents liked to call "fake-itis," and watching

Richard Simmons with his mother on morning television. Some of the members of the studio audience admitted to eating mayonnaise sandwiches in the past, and Richard berated them in a playful and loving way. He put his hands on his firm hips and shook his head in exaggerated disappointment. He then shook a schoolteacher's finger at them and said, "That's very very bad bad bad!" He was smiling, though, and ready to love everybody and exercise, and Perry wished that Richard Simmons was his schoolteacher. That day, as soon as his mother went into the shower, Perry stole for the kitchen and made his very first mayonnaise sandwich. He had never realized that two slices of Wonder Bread with nothing but mayo between them could taste so divine, and he had continued the luscious habit into early adulthood. "Thank you Richard Simmons," Perry thought.

A sudden noise from outside made Perry jump. His heart began to pound and he held his breath for a moment. He hopped to the window over the kitchen sink and peered out, straining to see as much as possible. The driveway was empty but it was impossible from the angle to see inside the McMillens' garage. "They couldn't already be home," Perry thought. "Shit!" He took no chances, however, and began to hide all evidence of the raid he had made on the refrigerator; on food that he had not only failed to pay for but that he had never been given permission to touch. Perry launched the steak knife into the sink and grabbed the loaf of pumpernickel. "Where's the fucking tie . . . where's the tie . . . oh shit." Perry fell to his knees and scoured the floor for any sign of the small piece of plastic. He swept his hands across every inch of tiling in his range, ignoring the dozens of tiny crumbs collecting on his sweaty palms, and continued to talk to himself. "I'm going to look like such an idiot!" Finally, under the kitchen table, Perry found the tie and he sprung to his feet to continue the cover up. His fingers felt frostbitten as he fumbled to tie up the bread bag. "How am I ever going to face them?" he wondered. "Shit!"

He heard the slamming of car doors and knew only seconds remained for him to get out of the kitchen. He screwed the tops on the mustard, mayonnaise, and the Hellman's Dijonnaise and stuffed them into the fridge. In his mind's eye, Perry could see Tanya and her parents, getting out of the car, Mrs. McMillen holding a bag with the new bottle of wine in it, Mr. McMillen tinkering with something in the garage before going inside, and Tanya, his beautiful girlfriend, making her way to the house. "She's going to see me!" Perry was running out of time so he flung the lettuce, mortadella, pickle jar, alfalfa sprouts, and turkey back into the fridge and hid the unwrapped mozzarella at the bottom of the garbage can next to the unused portion of the tomato he had stolen. "I'm a fucking thief!"

With the muffled voices of the McMillen family growing closer and louder by the second, Perry brushed the bread crumbs and tomato residue off the cutting board with his hand, sucked the sorry excuse for bruschetta from his fingers, grabbed the uncompleted sandwich and the blue towel, and ran for the bathroom. He got the shower going immediately and stripped himself of his Kentucky Fried Chicken uniform. Perry was panting but enjoying the return of oxygen to his lungs along with the gradual alleviation of his fear and panic from the kitchen. "I made it . . . I can't believe I fucking made it," he muttered to himself. He looked at the sandwich in his hand. "If only I had put some turkey in first! Shit!" Resigned to the fact that his meal was nothing more than a glorified cheese sandwich with a few slices of tomato, a little mustard and some Hellman's Dijonnaise spread, Perry hopped into the shower. He pushed the nozzle straight down, so as to not wet his sandwich. "Christ, I could have had two of these if they hadn't came back so fast," he thought. "I won't even be able to smoke now!"

There was knocking at the bathroom door. "How's it going in there, babe?" Tanya asked.

"Just fine," Perry composed himself. "I just have to wash my bum." He heard Tanya giggle on the other side of the door.

A bar of soap on a small shelf almost directly beneath the shower nozzle succumbed to the water pressure and slipped into the tub. Perry's instincts told him to bend over immediately and pick up the bar since soap melted faster when exposed to water. His father had taught him that at an early age and concern for melting soap came as naturally to Perry as the impulse to get out of the way of a speeding car did. He thought of a joke his father had told him when he was young, probably around the same time that he learned about melting soap.

Two bears were taking a bath. One said to the other, "Please pass the soap." The other looked around and said, "No soap, radio!"

This was a joke designed to be a real joke on the listener. It was best told with a collaborator; someone who knew about the joke and would feign wholehearted laughter after the impotent "No soap, radio" punchline. If the listener was weak-minded enough to laugh along even though he or she did not "get" the joke, the joke teller and the collaborator could then laugh at the listener. Perhaps Perry's father was trying to teach his son a lesson about being a follower, about the pitfalls of going along with the crowd. He had miscalculated, however, since the image of two bears taking a bath together was genuinely funny to Perry's eight-year-old esthetic sensibilities. He grew impatient and frustrated when his father attempted to explain why the joke was "really" funny. Since then Perry had been haunted by the lines of a very stupid joke every time he saw a bar of soap unnecessarily melting in water.

Perry turned his face away, leaving the soap bar to drown in the base of the tub, and began to concentrate on his pitiful sandwich. He pivoted so the water splashed on the back of his legs and took a bite. "Not enough mayo," he thought. Chewing with his mouth open, Perry looked the sandwich over. "Maybe Tanya will have sex with me in the car tonight," he thought. "Do I have enough cash, just in case, for the Motel Ideal?" Just then Perry spat out his half-chewed mouthful and gagged and coughed. It was not the thought of his girlfriend naked that made him act in such a disgusting manner, however. It was something about the sandwich. In his nonchalant inspection of the bread, Perry had discovered a horrifying defect.

Mould! Nauseated by the dusty green micro-organisms that had taken root on his sandwich and angered at the thought of having taken a terrible risk for nothing, Perry stomped one foot in the tub. Faced with the prospect of having to dispose of uneaten food, Perry heard the sound of his late grandmother's voice in his head. *Think of the poor, starving children in Cambodia, Perry.* He almost responded but shook himself back to reality. He had to get rid of the evidence but consuming it was now out of the question. There was a small garbage can in the washroom — perhaps he could hide it at the bottom of it as he had done with the cheese and tomato in the kitchen. But bathroom garbages never get changed, Perry pointed out to himself. He winced as a vision appeared in his mind of fruit flies hovering over the can and Mr. McMillen attempting to solve the mystery. Impulsively, Perry opened the shower curtain and plunked the sandwich into the toilet. He had one foot on the bath mat and one hand on the flusher when he realized that flushing a sandwich down the toilet not only stood a good chance of causing a blockage, but that it would also make his shower scalding hot for a few minutes. He reached into the toilet, withdrew the soppy moulded sandwich, and returned to the shower.

Perry crouched down and began to break up the sandwich into little, olive-sized pieces. He placed each one into the tub's drain. He had to keep pushing the bar of soap aside, as the sucking action of the drain continuously drew it toward the hole. He waited a few seconds before depositing each new sandwich morsel into the hole to be sure the last one had really gone down. "I look like the most pitiful person on Earth," Perry said to himself. He thought about all the dead people he knew who might be watching him now as ghosts. As a youngster, he had always been compelled to curb his behaviour around his grandmother, but now that she was dead did that mean he had to be good all the time? "She couldn't be here now, I'm naked," Perry assured himself. He returned to the task at hand, hoping his plan would work. It took about five minutes to dispose of the entire sandwich, piece by piece, down the bathtub's drainpipe. There was another knock at the door.

"Almost done in there, Perry? We'd like you to be dry by the time we get to my sister's house." It was Mr. McMillen. Perry laughed out of courteous instinct but paranoia made him answer as one would a drill sergeant.

"Be out in a sec!"

Perry wet his hair and grabbed a plastic bottle of shampoo from the shelf beneath the shower nozzle. He quickly lathered his armpits with the triple-action formula to alleviate some of the odour from his day's work, rinsed, and turned the water off. He stepped out of the shower and dried himself with the fluffy blue towel. Perry wondered what he was supposed to do with somebody else's towel after he had used it. At home, he simply placed his towels back on a hook and his mother would eventually put them in the wash when she felt they had been used enough. Here, though, nobody would be using the towel again before laundry day so he felt a little guilty about hanging it up in the bathroom. While his father had taught him many things about the physical properties of soap, he had failed to instill any sort of guest towel etiquette in his son. Perry had no choice but to hang the towel up but, out of politeness and consideration, was careful not to let it touch the other McMillen towels on the rack.

He put his good clothes on and left the bathroom. Mr. McMillen was still waiting outside and the two smiled uncomfortably at each other. Tanya appeared from around a corner and gave him a big hug around the neck. "Let's go in my room and do your hair," she said. She planted a big kiss on his cheek with her soft lips, wetting them on Perry's damp skin. "I like it when you comb it down." Perry was rigid, he felt ill at ease with one of Tanya's parents so close by. They began to walk down the hall.

The voice came from back inside the bathroom. "What did you do to my bathtub, Perry?" Mr. McMillen asked half-jokingly and half-annoyed. Perry was silent. He had no sarcastically friendly comeback for Tanya's father this time; he was unable to utter a word. "Looks like you blocked up my bathtub. It's full of water. Are you shedding or something?"

The sandwich! The plan hadn't worked and Mr. McMillen was on the verge of discovering Perry's act of robbery. In that moment Perry wished more than ever that his body could follow his mind to some remote town in northern Manitoba where polar bears come in the spring to feast in the garbage dumps. Maybe he would be one of the lucky citizens to be interviewed by the reporters from the big cities who flocked annually to the town to take advantage of this cute human-interest story. Perry thought that he'd like to give his opinion that the yearly polar bear visit was nothing and it was the media invasion alone that caused the biggest disturbances to his little town for a few days every year. He wondered which television station would be brave enough to air his dissenting views on the matter. His body was firmly grounded in the McMillen hallway, however, and his continental wandering was cut off by the voice of the father of the house.

"Why don't you come in here and give me a hand unblocking this thing, Perry."

He wanted, needed, to run. He only stood there.

Tanya pushed him toward the bathroom. "Go and help him, babe."

"Better yet," Mr. McMillen began again, "you can go get my tool box from the garage. It looks like I might need a screwdriver or something to fish out whatever's blocking all this water."

"Why . . . why don't you just try some Liquid Drano or something, Mr. McMillen?" Perry practically pleaded.

"I don't like to put too much of that stuff into the pipes. It eats them all up."

Perry wouldn't have minded a little Drano to eat his own insides up at that moment. Anything would have been better than facing Mr. McMillen and Tanya once the remnants of his sandwich were extracted. There would be no way to explain it away. He made for the garage, hoping Tanya would stay with her father and he could run. Run away and never come back. Hiding was better than humiliation and there would be no humiliation as long as Perry was hiding. True to form, however, Tanya followed him to get her father's tool box. "You don't mind helping him, eh Perry?"

"Ah, no. No, not at all." Perry thought he might push Tanya down and run, but he stopped himself. Doing that would mean giving up everything he had or would ever have with Tanya. He was torn. He feared the censure of the lips as much as he loved them. Why did he always do things like this?

They retrieved the tool box together. It was a giant red thing made of metal with three sets of fold-out shelves and Perry felt it weighed a ton. The box boasted every tool a family could ever need; screwdrivers, hammers, pliers, a giant wrench perfect for taking pipes apart, to name but a few. There were even a few gems still wrapped in unopened packages; four extra bolts for keeping the toilet bowl connected to the floor, a tiny rock sculpting hammer, and a pair of UV-protective work goggles; every tool a family could never need.

Perry and Tanya made their way back to the washroom. Perry feared it might be the last thing they would ever do together. Mr. McMillen was sitting on the edge of the tub. Perry thought he might know already. He would have liked very much to use the toilet. "I don't know what the hell's in there. I can't see through this water, it's all murky." Relief. For the moment. Small beads of sweat tickled Perry's forehead and his hands shook slightly, causing the tool box to rattle a bit. Tanya's father was frustrated and getting impatient, and he took it out on his daughter. "Tanya, are you helping or watching?" She looked surprised. "Will you please wait outside?" Tanya stomped off.

Now the men were alone. Time to roll up the sleeves and get to the bottom of things. Only Perry already knew exactly why the bathtub was blocked. The water would not go down because Perry had to have a little extra; he wasn't satisfied with what he was being offered; he had to have more. He had never been satisfied and probably never would. "And what did I get?" he asked himself, knowing the answer. "A moulded sandwich with no mayo and no meats and a blocked tub to expose me." He felt a sudden urge to confess. Perhaps full admission of guilt before disclosure would at least gain Perry a little respect even if it did nothing for the shame.

The words were on the tip of Perry's tongue when Mr. McMillen got down on his knees with his back to him. He looked at the man's hunched shoulders and listened to the sounds of splashing water. "Just tell him, get it over with," Perry told himself. He grabbed the large wrench from the tool box instead.

The small bald spot on the back of Mr. McMillen's head looked putty soft to Perry. He would not face the humiliation, he had to avoid it. It occurred to Perry, in the moment that he began to raise the wrench in the air, that Clue games don't have bathrooms. They have Halls, Conservatories, and Kitchens, and they certainly have Wrenches, but no Lavatories. Perhaps there were no famous crimes or murders that took place in a washroom to inspire the creators of Clue.

The wrench was high above Perry's head and he knew that running to a canning town in New Brunswick would be worth the trouble if he could prevent Mr. McMillen from discovering the dissected sandwich in his drain pipe. Living on the lam never looked so good to Perry and he actually began to look forward to his new life on the run. "I'll only have to be really careful for five, maybe six years," he thought. Perry felt the cold steel of the wrench handle press against the small bones in his fingers, felt the heat of straining tendons in his forearm as they struggled to keep the heavy tool aloft. He began to swing the wrench. "Will it crack? Will it crunch?" he wondered.

A terrifically loud sucking sound suddenly filled the air in the bathroom. It startled Perry so much that he missed his target, struck himself on the knee, and dropped the wrench onto the back of Mr. McMillen's left calf. Perry slumped to the ground, his right kneecap throbbing. Mr. McMillen let out a sharp yelp and scrambled to his feet. The sucking didn't stop and Perry thought for a second that his grandmother was returning from the dead to tell him how naughty he had been and that there would be no more chocolate bars until his behaviour changed. Mr. McMillen returned Perry to the reality of his surroundings:

"Goddammit! What are you fooling with a wrench for, Perry?"

Perry ignored his girlfriend's father's words. He only listened to the sucking and swishing sounds that he now realized were emanating from the tub. Mr. McMillen was sweating and screaming and waving one arm in the air, but his words were no more discernible to Perry than the speech of the schoolteacher in *Peanuts* television cartoon specials. The sweet sucking. That was what Perry was interested in. "The . . . the water! Is it going down?" Perry cried.

Mr. McMillen rubbed the back of his leg. "Yes it's going down, you klutz!" He threw a small bar of wet soap at Perry. "There's the problem. There's the damned blockage. A piece of soap. Don't you put the soap back when you're finished? Oh, my leg!"

Perry felt giddy with relief. It was as if he had just finished a ten-hour shift in the Kentucky Fried Chicken kitchen and had the next two weeks off. He shuffled to his good knee to watch the last swirl of water sink down into the drain. It looked like a tiny tornado. "It's okay? The tub's okay?"

"The tub's okay. The tub's okay," Mr. McMillen mocked, imitating the frenzy in Perry's voice. He wondered why Perry was so distraught but attributed it to his prior conviction that the boy was simply strange. "The tub's okay but soap isn't cheap, you know. It melts a hell of a lot faster if you leave it in the water. Don't you think you could be a little more careful there, Perry?"

Perry eyed the fallen wrench again as he stood up. He gripped it. He handed it to Mr. McMillen. The man shook it at Perry, feigned a swing in the air, and smiled.

No soap, radio.

HANGING MURRAY

Ripples of pleasant sickness lapped against the insides of Murray's stomach as, to his complete surprise and through little real effort of his own, he was actually getting somewhere with Linda from Accounting.

Five of the more inebriated had banded together after the office Christmas party broke up and found a bar to keep drinking in. The music wasn't particularly loud but Linda spoke to Murray as if it was, drawing him near and enunciating directly into his ear, warm lips brushing against his lobe every now and then. When he spoke back she leaned way in and the scent of tobacco in her hair so close to his nose emphasized just how private their conversation was becoming. Knees touched under the table and she did not pull away.

He didn't see them walk into the place, perhaps they'd been there the whole time, but Murray suddenly noticed Nicodemus and Karsten Kounekakis leaning against the bar side by side, wide butts in matching pairs of Wrangler jeans. Old schoolmates of Murray's, Nico and Karsten were often mistaken for twins because they were in the same class. Nico, however, was the elder sibling who had failed Grade 3 twice.

Their family owned the neighbourhood pizzeria, Buono Bruno, and Nico and Karsten were the fattest kids in school. Murray spent an inordinate portion of his gym classes mesmerized by the flapping waddle of flesh that hung beneath their T-shirts as they chased basketballs, floor hockey pucks, and soccer balls. They perspired like adults; beads of sweat traced lines down their plump faces, dripped onto the gymnasium floor; dark patches of dampness appeared beneath their arms and along their midriffs. They had mustaches — thin ones, but mustaches in primary school nonetheless. The brothers never seemed to notice they looked out of place.

Which is exactly what Murray thought when he saw Nico and Karsten at the bar, chubby fingers of their olive-toned hands wrapped around the necks of Bud bottles: out of place. Linda and her advances was still his primary focus; now when she laughed she'd slap *his* knee instead of her own and allow her hand to linger. But seeing the Kounekakis brothers and their wet, involuntarily pouting lips and greasy black mullets among a sea of workout-worshipping, fashion-conscious bar hoppers was messing with his concentration, throwing him off of his game.

In grade school, Murray excelled in one, very particular, area: the flexed arm hang. He got average grades, minor roles in school plays, and shied away from student government, but Murray could hang from a bar, hands in line with his eyes, far longer than anyone in his class could. He looked forward to the annual school-wide fitness tests the way other kids looked forward to summer vacation. And every year he got closer to being in Grade 6, when the names of the top students in each fitness category were embossed on a big plaque beside the gymnasium door, immortalized. Young Murray lay awake in the dark on many nights, envisioning his name alongside the names of great flexed arm hangers who came before him. He imagined the distinction would eventually play some kind of a role in earning him a wife. He imagined how he'd show the plaque to the children she'd bear him.

In the week leading up to the competition Murray tried to get his friends to call him "Hanging Murray," but they teased him for it. He barely noticed, too blinded by the aura of destiny.

He almost laughed when Nico Kounekakis wrapped the chubby fingers of his olive-toned hands around the hanging bar to his left on fitness test day. Their eyes met and he saw Nico sigh with arched eyebrows, conceding not just defeat, but utter ineptness to the task at hand. Murray found himself looking Nico in the face, and not the stomach, for the first time. He heard wheezing to his right and turned to see Karsten taking the other spot next to him. Somebody yelled out there was a new sandwich on the menu at Buono Bruno, and Murray was the meat between Nico and Karsten's buns. The whole gymnasium laughed. Murray watched Karsten, but he only stared at the hanging bar, looking half asleep, like he just wanted the whole thing over with.

The whistle blew and Murray suspended himself in the air with only the strength of his biceps. He felt the old, familiar effortlessness — easy as spreading butter on toast. Actually winning was a mere formality.

Maybe twenty seconds in a terrible stench invaded Murray's nostrils. Like rotting cold cuts and orange rinds, like chewing gum and chicken broth, like taco powder and diapers — or something eerily in between them all — the odour pushed deeper into his respiratory system. Trembling, he found himself powerless to take a breath. He glanced at Nico, who was hanging with his arms stretched straight, sweat staining black through the armpits of his T-shirt, rocking back and forth, teeth clenched. The reek grew stronger and Murray had to turn his head the other way, in Karsten's direction, whose arms weren't flexed at all, either. Slick black armpit hairs snaked out from his T-shirt sleeves. Murray's lungs burned. He had to breathe but his offended nose wouldn't allow it. He dropped. No plaque for Murray. He was mortal.

Murray put his arm around Linda's shoulder and started to laugh. She stiffened at his sudden move but allowed it. He leaned toward her ear and told her to look over at the bar.

"Those guys," he giggled. "Look at them!" He felt drunker than ever. He saw Nico reach behind himself and scratch his left buttock, oblivious. Murray was beside himself. "Oh my God, look at them! Those two! I know those two!"

Linda laughed, getting into it, hand on his knee again. "From where?"

Murray cackled. "Those guys," he paused to try and control his laughter, clear his throat. "Those guys — " he couldn't stop laughing but blurted it out: "Those are the four smelliest armpits in all of Montreal!"

Murray slipped off his chair and fell to his knees, laughing. His head shook back and forth and he crowed, repeating, "The smelliest armpits!" over and over. He leaned forward, hands on the floor, wetness and crumbs on his palms, laughing, all the time laughing.

He regained his chair eventually. Linda wasn't talking into his ear anymore. Her hands lay dormant, folded on top of the table. She wasn't really looking at him at all, and her conversation included everyone again, not him alone.

When the police entered Murray's condo just before five o'clock that morning they found a half-eaten pot of

Kraft Dinner and a crusted fork on the living room floor, the television tuned to scrambled porn, and the balcony door wide open. They reported the death as an accident when they found a slight outward bend in the steel bar of the balcony railing. "Idiot must've been hanging from it," one detective surmised out on the balcony, shaking her head and tracing the bend with her gloved forefinger. "Must've been hanging for a damned long time."

LOOKING THE PART

There was only one Maple Boston left. Carl wet the edge of his finger with his tongue and dabbed the fallen coconut slivers and chocolate sprinkles from the bottom of the Tim Hortons box before grabbing it. "You wanna split it?"

Jeremy opened his eyes to slits and looked up at him pitiably from the kitchen floor. He scratched under his chin, scratched short beard bristles. "I can't. I'll be sick."

"Have another potato, then. At least one more."

"No more. Just let me sleep." Jeremy took a deep breath and let out an apneatic sigh, closed his eyes. The lower portion of his potbelly was exposed, heaving with every breath, untucked white undershirt pulled up slightly. Stretch marks, like purplish-blue drips of rain on a windowpane, lined the sides of his trunk. Sleep seemed to come instantly.

Carl bit into the Maple Boston, nibbled around the edges as he turned the donut round and round in his hands, saved the custard-filled centre for last.

He stood up from the kitchen table, decided he'd clean up in the morning, after seeing Jeremy off to his shoot. He was too full to do anything now. He went to the living room and grabbed a cushion from the couch, took it back to the kitchen. He put one hand under his younger brother's head and lifted it from the floor, shoved the cushion beneath it. Jeremy coughed but didn't wake up.

Carl glanced at the table, strewn with empty beer bottles, banana peels, olive pits, the date squares that were too stale and old to eat, the crusting pasta bowl from the spaghetti and meatballs, potato skins, 10% cream cartons, and donut crumbs.

He sighed. He flicked the kitchen light off and thought, "We should have just gone to a buffet."

The Pizza Hut was their mother's automatic choice to celebrate Jeremy's latest triumph in. It was where they had always gone as a family, especially when the kids were growing up. Carl couldn't remember exactly how many Pizza Hut birthday parties he'd had as a kid, there'd been so many, but suspected Jeremy had had more.

Once, over drinks, Carl told Jeremy that he believed their mother couldn't see beyond the Pizza Hut.

"No," Jeremy said, "I think she just likes the Pizza Hut."

"I'll see you tomorrow."

Carl showed up late on purpose. He didn't want to see his mother hug and fawn over his brother at first sight, or see his father stand to the side with his hands clasped together in front of his stomach, salivating at the anticipation of congratulating the prodigal son. And Alex. He wanted to spend as little time as possible in the presence of Alex. Maybe if she ever got off her ass and actually moved out of their parents' house he'd gain some kind of respect for her. She even smoked in front of them now, and they didn't do anything about it.

Carl paused between the front entrance and the gumball machine. He spied his family crammed into a booth in the smoking section. An empty chair waited for him at the short outer edge of the table. The hostess greeted him with a menu in her hand. She wore more foundation on her cheeks and forehead than a corpse, black lipstick and eyeliner. Carl had seen her many times before; the family privately referred to her as "the vampire," though he suspected his father never really caught on and only pretended to know who they were talking about.

"Your family is sitting over there," the vampire said, pointing.

"Thanks."

Carl walked over and rested his hand on the back of his chair.

"Hello. Carl," his father said in that whacko, robotic pacing that drove Carl crazy but wasn't allowed to complain about anymore on orders from his mother. "Do. You. Like. Stuffed. Crust. Pizza?"

"Anything's fine," he replied, tersely. "Hi everyone." He looked around the table. Jeremy and their mother were engrossed in conversation. Alex butted out a cigarette in the aluminum ashtray and closed her eyes. His father gazed at the menu, eyebrows raised in fascination.

"How. About. Bread. Sticks? Do. You. Think. Five. Is. A. Good. Amount. Or. Should. We. Get. Ten?"

"Have a pill or two extra this morning, Dad?"

"Carl!"

"Hi, Mom." He stared at her, daring her with his eyes to scold him, her thirty-year-old son. His mother's skin was pale with scraggly lines of wrinkles around her eyes and mouth. Her eyes looked wet all the time now.

The click and flash of Alex's lighter put an end to the showdown, and she blew a column of smoke between them for good measure. Carl caught Jeremy staring at him through the haze, and his brother furrowed his eyebrows, asking "why?" silently. Carl looked away, focused on his father.

"Five's probably best. Five breadsticks, Dad. Jeremy has to watch his weight."

"Not this time!" their mother exclaimed proudly. "The casting director told him to put on a few pounds for this one."

"A few pounds," Carl repeated vaguely, trying hard not to tell his mother to wipe the stupid grin off her face.

"Actually it's more like twenty," Jeremy said.

"*Twenty* pounds?" their mother cried out, drawing a quick sideways weave of the head from a woman at the table across from them. "That's too much, Jeremy."

"Wow. What. A. Challenge."

"Shut up, Allen," their mother reproved. "Jeremy, you tell them no. You'll do the commercial the way you are."

"This should be good," Alex said without breathing through her nose, little puffs of smoke escaping her mouth with each syllable.

The waiter arrived.

"We'd. Like. To. Start. With. Twenty. Bread. Sticks. Please."

Carl and Jeremy, as was their custom, made for the Typhoon Lounge after the family dinner for their requisite two, three or nine drinks after exposure to their mother, father, and sister.

They grabbed a spot near the back of the bar. Before taking off his coat, Carl removed a brand new pack of Du Maurier Lights from an inside pocket, tossed it on the table. Jeremy unwrapped it, crumpled the cellophane into the ashtray, and took out two cigarettes, handed one to Carl. A waitress with black roots showing through her blond hair arrived, clutching an empty tray to her side. Carl looked up at her. "Two vodka crans. Doubles. And some matches, please." He placed the cigarette between the edges of his lips, held it there gently, dangling, waiting for a light, confident their mother would never walk into a place like the Typhoon.

"Anxious for one?" Jeremy asked, pointing at Carl's cigarette with his chin.

"Aren't you?"

"I don't know how Alex does it."

"Because she doesn't care about anything. She doesn't give a fuck."

"And she probably never will." Jeremy leaned back straight against his chair, thrust both hands into his pants pockets. "Get over it. You and me, we're hypocrites." He produced a lighter from his left pocket and held out an open flame for Carl.

The waitress placed their drinks on the table, ice clinking against the sides of the glasses. "You still want these?" she asked, a book of matches between her thumb and forefinger.

"Yeah, I'll take them," Carl said. "Please."

They were left to their drinks. Silence for a moment. Carl stared at Jeremy's face without looking directly into his eyes, marvelled at how much they resembled each other. Separated by only twenty months in age, they had the same hairline, receded pointy widow's peaks, same round, large eyes, brown, and the same dark circles beneath them. Only the zits that still materialized on Carl's forehead every now and then and Jeremy's thin goatee really distinguished them. Carl felt Jeremy returning his stare and said the first thing that came to mind, "She's kind of cute," turning to look back at the waitress.

Jeremy acknowledged his comment with a quiet grunt. "I really don't know what I'm going to do about this part."

"I might not agree much with Mom, but I think it's pretty ridiculous, too."

"It's what they want." Jeremy sounded defeated. "And if I want the part—"

"Yeah, but do you really need it?"

"My agent says I do."

"Maybe you could make an even bigger name for yourself by saying no. You know, 'Jeremy Clarke turned down a hardware store commercial because they asked him to gain weight.' You know, make a reputation for yourself."

"I'd be making a *bad* reputation," Jeremy said, and took a sip of his drink. "You don't understand. It doesn't work that way. Not in real life, anyway. They say I don't look fat enough to be a hardware customer, I'm not believable, so I have to get fatter."

Carl was quiet for a moment, dragged on his cigarette. He culled his natural instinct to lash out at his brother for not agreeing with him, went the controlled, soft route. "Sorry. I was just trying to help."

"That's okay," Jeremy said, incredulous. "I have to figure out some kind of a regimen."

"It shouldn't be too hard. Just eat a lot."

"It sounds easy, I know, but I talked to this guy who had to do it once. He said he had to get somebody to help him. Like a sponsor."

"A sponsor?"

"What about you, Carl? Help me put on twenty pounds?"

Carl had his brother move in with him temporarily, the easier to feed him. Jeremy gave him $110 for food, not nearly enough for three weeks of gorging, but promised to pay him back when the royalties started coming in once the commercial went to air. Carl supplemented the food budget himself, not the first time he'd sacrificed for his brother's sake, but took to being Jeremy's personal chef and eating coach, feeling rather happy to contribute so directly to his acting career.

He placed large bowls strategically around the apartment: in the hallway, the living room, even the bathroom, and filled them with cheesies, cashews, pretzels, and other snack fare. He stocked up on bread, Kraft Singles, and taco sauce — from growing up together, Carl knew the one snack Jeremy could never resist was melted cheese on bread with taco sauce. He figured he could sneak a couple slices of ham under the cheese, and Jeremy's waistline would be the better for it. He prepared spaghetti sauces thick with ground beef, the fattiest ground beef he could buy, and he didn't drain the grease. He filled the fruit bowl with bananas, dates, and walnuts, with a nutcracker nearby. After only a few days he was so engrossed in the project that he stopped wondering what he might get out of the whole affair for himself.

After seven days Jeremy was only four pounds heavier, with two weeks to go before the filming. "You're not eating enough," Carl said, laying floppy strips of lasagna in his big casserole dish. "You have to eat this whole lasagna. Tonight."

"But I'm not even hungry now," Jeremy whined. He halfheartedly rummaged through a bowl of barbecue chips on the kitchen table, extracted one, put it back. "I think I better just call my agent. Tell him to forget it. I can't do it."

"You can't give up now," Carl said, spreading cottage cheese over the pasta with a spoon.

"No, really. I can't do it. I'm going to call."

A sensation of fear, loss, struck Carl in the back of his shoulders and neck. He dropped his spoon in the saucepot.

"They'll get pissed off at you. You'll get blacklisted. Come on, if you can't eat the whole lasagna, eat three-quarters of it, then. At least that."

"I can't!"

"You have to!"

"Okay, I'll make you a deal," Jeremy said, pushing the chip bowl further away from him. "You eat half of it and I'll eat half of it."

"I'm not the one who has to put on weight."

"Yeah, but if you do it it'll make it easier for me. Please, Carl?"

Carl ladled a big scoop of sauce, a sauce inundated with ground beef, shredded chicken, and pork. He poured it atop the cottage cheese, then reached for more lasagna strips. "Okay. Just this once."

Carl showed up after work one night with six McDonald's bags, their top flaps rolled up under the curled fingers of both his hands. The scent of mustard and beef followed him into the apartment, rolled in on an invisible fast food fog.

"You know, when I was a kid I always dreamed of doing this," he said, excited, handing Jeremy half the bags.

"What?"

"Going through the Drive Thru and ordering thirty small cheeseburgers and ten small hamburgers."

Jeremy's eyes widened and he fingered one of the bags open, peered inside with his chin tucked tight against his chest. "This is what we're eating tonight?"

"I don't feel like cooking. But listen to me, Jer! I just lived out a childhood fantasy! I remember I used to think, especially when I was mad at Mom or Dad, 'One day nobody will be able to tell me what to do, nobody's going to be the boss of me. I'll be an adult and I'll be able to do whatever I want. Nobody will be able to stop me from going through the McDonald's Drive Thru and ordering thirty small cheeseburgers if I wanted!' Jer, *thirty cheeseburgers*! I did it!"

"And ten hamburgers, right? You said you got ten hamburgers."

"Yeah, yeah. Ten."

"Why thirty-ten?" Jeremy asked, unwrapping a hamburger. "Why not twenty of each, half and half?" He took a bite.

"I like cheeseburgers best. But I also like hamburgers. Just not as much."

Jeremy chewed and spoke at the same time. "So that's like your ratio?"

"Ratio?"

"You like small cheeseburgers three times as much as you like small hamburgers. Thirty cheeseburgers, ten hamburgers."

"Yeah, I guess."

"That's too bad."

"Why?"

"I like hamburgers best."

At the end of week two, Carl was still frustrated with Jeremy's progress. He'd taken on five more pounds, only a slight improvement over the first week's results, and he was still behind schedule: one week to go and eleven more pounds to gain. Carl was also discouraged by the fact that the scope of their half-and-half agreement over the lasagna had expanded, and now applied to *every* meal. Jeremy refused to eat anything unless Carl ate an equal portion and it was showing. At work guys were teasing Carl and sneaking up behind him to try and pinch an inch.

Despite his slow progress, Jeremy definitely looked bigger than the night of the Pizza Hut celebration. Alex said as much when she popped in for a visit. "Oh my god," she snorted, coming in the door. "What a porker!"

Carl left the kitchen to greet his sister, spied her feet. "Alex! Please! Your shoes!"

"Chill," she hissed. Then her cheeks puffed up full of air, eyes wide. She burst out laughing, pointed at Carl. "What, are you trying out for a part, too? Forget Fat Elvis. Here's Fat Carl!"

"Shut up, Alex, and take your shoes off," Carl barked. "This isn't easy to do, you know."

"Yeah, maybe. But you certainly seem to be enjoying it."

Alex stayed for dinner — tacos and burritos with rice and refried beans — had too much beer, and announced after refusing a slice of cheesecake that she'd be sleeping over. Carl and Jeremy shared a private look of disappointment and went to work on dividing the cake.

In the living room, *Star Trek* on the TV, "Amok Time," Alex sat on the floor, her back against the couch. Face flushed, she laughed at Kirk and Spock fighting, cigarette ash teetering between her fingers. Jeremy was curled up in one corner of the couch, a bowl of Doritos between his stomach and knees, reciting lines. Carl, on the other side of the couch, had Jeremy's hardware script in his hands, checking lines. Captain Kirk, on his knees, heaved giant breaths of thin Vulcan air into his exhausted lungs. Alex laughed even harder and threw her head back against the couch, kicked her feet in the air.

"Alex, come on!" Carl snapped. "Don't exaggerate."

Alex ashed into an empty beer bottle and turned around. "Fuck off. Fatso."

Carl reached across the couch and swatted his sister with Jeremy's script.

"Both of you stop it!" Jeremy yelled. "I'm trying to learn my lines!"

"Yeah, Alex," Carl added. "You're not helping us here."

"Us?" she laughed. "Us? What's this 'us'?"

"We're trying to get ready for the commercial, stupid," Carl said, straightening the script out.

"We? *Jeremy's* in the commercial, Carl. Not you. You're his cook. Don't get all high and mighty on me. I'm not taking that shit from Jeremy's cook."

Carl shot up from the couch and threw the script down, stormed from the room. He slapped the doorframe on the way into the kitchen and sat down at the table. It was a mess. Dinner and dessert plates already crusting, still scattered about. Little orange shreds of cheddar cheese hardening on the table's smooth surface. Empty beer bottles. Jeremy's pack of cigarettes. Carl grabbed one and lit up.

Jeremy entered the room. "Don't listen to her."

"But she's right."

Jeremy sighed, looked around. "No."

"Don't try to make me feel better."

"I'm not. I'm telling the truth. Everybody thinks it's all glamorous for me but they're wrong. You're the one I look up to. And deep down, Alex probably does, too."

"Jer, my life is boring. I sell cheese for a living."

"That's beautiful."

The day after Alex's visit Carl was on the road, a two-hour gap between meetings with clients. He lived out his childhood Drive Thru fantasy for the second time in ten days, alone this time, parked in a desolate spot behind the McDonald's, unobstructed view of the big air-conditioning unit, trying out Jeremy's half and half cheeseburger to hamburger ratio this time, found he could only get through six of each. He opened his glove compartment and emptied it of maps, gas receipts, a cassette copy of Rush's *A Farewell to Kings* (which made him realize it had been too long since he'd heard "Xanadu"), a green pen, and a tire gauge. He replaced these items with the remaining cheeseburgers and hamburgers, stacking them neatly in two rows, four stacks to a row, and four burgers in each back row stack, three in each in the front row. It looked like his own personal McDonald's bin — for true authenticity he was only missing the little, L-shaped metal clips the managers used to supposedly keep track of how long the burgers sat for. He closed the glove compartment and opened it again, observing his collection, wondering how long a McDonald's small cheeseburger or hamburger could safely sit for. He'd avoid turning the heater on too high, he decided.

The phone rang, Carl answered. "Hello?"

"Jeremy? Jeremy is that you?" their mother's voice squawked through the receiver.

Carl paused for a second, trying to decide. "Yeah, it's me, Mom. Jeremy." The similarities between Carl and Jeremy did not end with their looks; they also had indistinguishable voices, fodder for many telephone jokes over the years.

"Why are you answering Carl's phone? He gets *business* calls, you know!"

Carl was pleasantly surprised — he hadn't heard his mother sticking up for him in a while. "Oh, well, you know, I've been staying here so long I've been answering the phone. Anyway, Carl's not here," Carl said, trying to sound laid-back, the way Jeremy spoke.

"He's not? It's eight o'clock. Where is he?"

"Oh, he said he had a *business* meeting."

"That's good. Look, I picked up your prescription — "

"Prescription?" Carl asked, forgetting to be natural.

" — and I can drop it off to you tomorrow." Their mother hadn't stopped talking. "You know you should have told me sooner, you're not supposed to miss a pill."

"Well, um . . . " Carl didn't know what to say.

"You don't have to be embarrassed about the money, Jeremy. I'd rather pay for it than have you skip your pills."

"Why?" Carl asked, too curious to worry about getting caught impersonating his brother. "What could happen?"

"Jeremy, don't be silly. You don't want to have a panic attack before your commercial, do you?"

"No. No, of course not," Carl said. He got a little cramp in the base of his stomach. "Mom, can I call you back in a little bit? I have to get a pie out of the oven."

Carl hung up the phone, took a deep breath. His cramp grew in intensity. He walked to the living room and shook Jeremy from his nap on the couch. "Mom wants you to call her." His brother opened his eyes but turned and buried his face in the couch cushions, settled back into sleep. Carl shook him again. "She said it was important."

On the night before the commercial shoot, Carl and Jeremy split eighteen beers over dinner and dessert: peanut butter sandwiches, steak and potatoes — lots of potatoes — and a box of Tim Hortons donuts.

After a few donuts, Jeremy weighed himself. To Carl it was sad to see him this way, drunk and potbellied, greasy-faced and a big red pimple on the tip of his nose, trying to keep his balance on the scale. The weight he'd gained showed itself mainly in his face and stomach. From certain angles, he didn't really appear fat; from others he looked gross. Unhealthy, but definitely looking the part. Carl had gone through a metamorphosis of his own; despite starting a week later, he'd caught up and surpassed Jeremy's size and weight.

"Two-o-two," Jeremy slurred. "I've put on eighteen."

"That's pretty damned close." Carl slapped his brother on the back.

"Any more beer?"

In the kitchen, Jeremy lay down on the floor, his tenth beer beside him. Carl sat at the table, lit a cigarette, offered one to Jeremy. "No thanks," he said, "I think I'm going to be sick."

"You better finish that beer. And don't forget you have to shave, too."

"I'm just going to take a little nap. I'll shave in a minute." Jeremy closed his eyes.

Carl placed his elbows on the table and clasped his hands together, cigarette sticking out between his fingers. He leaned his face in to smoke. He looked down at his brother. Lucky bastard, he thought. Tomorrow he'd be making a commercial while Carl was at work. He regretted all the beers he'd drunk, but regretted having a job even more. Jeremy had it good, Carl thought.

"Hey," he said, remembering his duty. "Wake up." Carl dragged the Tim Hortons box closer to him with a hooked finger. Just one Maple Boston left. He wet the edge of his finger with his tongue and dabbed the fallen coconut slivers and chocolate sprinkles from the bottom of the box before grabbing it. "You wanna split it?"

Jeremy vomited throughout the night. Carl helped him stay upright on his knees in front of the bowl. When their parents showed up in the morning to drive Jeremy to the shoot, he was white as a sheet and sweating, barely awake.

"What's *wrong* with him?" their mother asked, panic in her voice. "What went on here?"

Their father spied the mess in the kitchen. "Looks. Like. There. Was. A. Lot. Of. Eating. And. Drinking. Happening. Here." He turned to Carl. "And. Smoking?"

"We're taking him to the hospital," their mother announced. "This is not right."

"Mom," Carl chided, "he's got a commercial to shoot. He'll be fine. Don't be ridiculous."

"No. He's going right now."

They left, their father supporting Jeremy out the door. Jeremy didn't seem to know what was going on.

Carl alone. Three weeks of work for nothing. His own explosion in weight for nothing.

He found the script on the living room floor, carried it in his hand to the recycling bin. One last look before throwing it out. An address and call time scrawled across the top of the page. He didn't have to ask himself twice. Carl patted his potbelly and walked out the door, possibilities on his mind.

The author wishes to acknowledge the invaluable encouragement and criticism so generously provided by David Hansen-Miller, Martin Kevan, and all members of The Caravan Collective, without whom this collection of stories would not have been possible.

"Saturday Night" appeared in the anthology *Telling Stories: New English Fiction from Québec,* edited by Claude Lalumière (Véhicule Press), "Counting to Prettidase-Nine" appeared in *Sub-TERRAIN,* "Other People's Funerals" appeared in *Exile: The Literary Quarterly,* "Red Pants on Monkland" appeared in *Pottersfield Portfolio,* "Other People's Showers" appeared in the anthology *Career Suicide! Contemporary Literary Humour,* edited by Jon Paul Fiorentino (DC Books), "Hanging Murray" was electronically published by espressofiction.com.